Anne Thackeray

Beauty and The Beast. Cinderella. Little Red Riding Hood. The Sleeping Beauty in The Wood.

SALZWASSER
VERLAG

Anne Thackeray

Beauty and The Beast. Cinderella. Little Red Riding Hood. The Sleeping Beauty in The Wood.

1st Edition | ISBN: 978-3-75253-050-6

Place of Publication: Frankfurt am Main, Germany

Year of Publication: 2021

Salzwasser Verlag GmbH, Germany.

Reprint of the original, first published in 1867.

BEAUTY AND THE BEAST.

BY

MISS THACKERAY,

AUTHOR OF "THE VILLAGE ON THE CLIFF."

FROM "THE CORNHILL."

LORING, Publisher,
319 WASHINGTON STREET,
BOSTON.
1867.

BEAUTY AND THE BEAST.

I.

FAIRY times, gifts, music, and dances are said to be over; or, as it has been said, they come to us so disguised and made familiar by habit that they do not seem to us strange. H. and I, on either side of the hearth, these long past winter evenings could sit without fear of fiery dwarfs skipping out of the ashes, of black puddings coming down the chimney to molest us. The clock ticked, the window-pane rattled. It was only the wind. The hearth-brush remained motionless on its hook. Pussy, dozing on the hearth, with her claws quietly opening to the warmth of the blaze, purred on and never once startled us out of our usual placidity by addressing us in human tones. The children sleeping peacefully upstairs were not suddenly whisked away and changelings deposited in their cribs. If H. or I opened our mouths pearls and diamonds did not drop out of them; but neither did frogs and tadpoles fall from between our lips. The looking-glass, tranquilly reflecting the comfortable little sitting-room, and the stiff ends of H.'s cap-ribbons, spared us visions of wreathing clouds parting to reveal distant scenes of horror and treachery. Poor H.! I am not sure but that she would have gladly looked in a mirror in which she could have sometimes seen the images of those she loved; but our chimney-glass, with its gilt moulding and bright polished surface, reflects only such homely scenes as two old women at work by the fire, some little Indian children at play upon the rug, the door opening and Susan bringing in the tea-things. As for wishing-cloths and little boiling pots, and such like, we have discovered that instead of rubbing lamps, or spreading magic table-cloths upon the floor, we have but to ring an invisible bell (which is even less trouble), and a smiling genius in a white cap and apron brings in anything we happen to fancy. When the clock strikes twelve, H. puts up her work and lights her candle; she has not yet been transformed into a beautiful princess all twinkling with jewels, neither does a scullion ever stand before me in rags; she does not murmur farewell forever and melt through the key-hole, but "Good-night," as she closes the door. One night at twelve o'clock, just after she had left me, there was indeed a loud orthodox ring at the bell, which startled us both a little. H. came running down again without her cap; Susan appeared in great alarm from the kitchen. "It is the back-door bell, ma'am," said the girl, who had been sitting up over her new Sunday gown, but who was too frightened to see who was ringing.

I may as well explain that our little house is in a street, but that our back windows have the advantage of overlooking the grounds of the villa belonging to our good neighbor and friend Mr. Griffiths, in Castle Gardens, and that a door opens out of our little back garden into his big one, of which we are allowed to keep the key. This door had been a postern gate once upon a time, for a bit of the old wall of the park is still standing, against which our succeeding bricks have been piled. It was a fortunate chance for us when our old ivy-tree died and we found the quaint little doorway behind it. Old Mr. Griffiths was alive then, and when I told him of my discovery he good-naturedly cleared the way on his side, and so the oak turned once more upon its rusty hinges to let the children pass through, and the nurse-maid, instead of pages and secret emissaries and men-at-arms; and about three times a year young Mr. Griffiths stoops under the arch on his way to call upon us. I say young Mr. Griffiths, but I suppose he is over thirty

3

now, for it is more than ten years since his father died.

When I opened the door, in a burst of wind and wet, I found that it was Guy Griffiths who stood outside bareheaded in the rain, ringing the bell that winter night. "Are you up?" he said. "For heaven's sake come to my mother; she's fainted; her maid is away; the doctor doesn't come. I thought you might know what to do." And then he led the way through the dark garden, hurrying along before me.

Poor lady! when I saw her I knew that it was no fainting-fit, but a paralytic stroke, from which she might perhaps recover in time; I could not tell. For the present there was little to be done. The maids were young and frightened; poor Guy wanted some word of sympathy and encouragement. So far I was able to be of use. We got her to bed and took off her finery, — she had been out at a dinner-party, and had been stricken on her return home, — Guy had discovered her speechless in the library. The poor fellow, frightened and overcome, waited about, trying to be of help, but he was so nervous that he tumbled over us all, and knocked over the chairs and bottles in his anxiety, and was of worse than no use. His kind old shaggy face looked pale, and his brown eyes *ringed* with anxiousness. I was touched by the young fellow's concern, for Mrs. Griffiths had not been a tender mother to him. How she had snapped and laughed at him, and frightened him with her quick, sarcastic tongue and hard, un-motherlike ways! I wondered if she thought of this as she lay there cold, rigid, watching us with glassy, senseless eyes.

The payments and debts and returns of affection are at all times hard to reckon. Some people pay a whole treasury of love in return for a stone; others deal out their affection at interest; others again take everything, to the uttermost farthing, and cast into the ditch and go their way and leave their benefactor penniless and a beggar. Guy himself, hard-headed as he was, and keen over his ledgers in Moorgate Street, could not have calculated such sums as these. All that she had had to give, all the best part of her shallow store, poor Julia Griffiths had paid to her husband, who did not love her; to her second son, whose whole life was a sorrow to his parents. When he died she could never forgive poor Guy for living still, for being his father's friend and right hand, and sole successor. She had been a real mother to Hugh, who was gone; to Guy, who was alive still and patiently waiting to do her bidding, she had shown herself only a step-dame; and yet I am sure no life-devoted mother could have been more anxiously watched and tended by her son. Perhaps, — how shall I say what I mean? — if he had loved her more and been more entirely one with her now, his dismay would have been less, his power greater to bear her pain, to look on at her struggling agony of impotence. Even pain does not come between the love of people who really love.

The doctor came and went, leaving some comfort behind him. Guy sat up all that night burning logs on the fire in the dressing-room, out of the bedroom in which Mrs. Griffiths was lying. Every now and then I went in to him and found him sitting over the hearth shaking his great shaggy head, as he had a way of doing, and biting his fingers, and muttering, "Poor soul! poor mother!" Sometimes he would come in creaking on tiptoe; but his presence seemed to agitate the poor woman, and I was obliged to motion him back again. Once, when I went in and sat down for a few minutes in an arm-chair beside him, he suddenly began to tell me that there had been trouble between them that morning. "It made it very hard to bear," he said.

I asked him what the trouble had been.

"I told her I thought I should like to marry," Guy confessed, with a rueful face. Even then I could hardly help smiling.

"Selfish beast that I am! I upset her, poor soul! I behaved like a brute."

His distress was so great that it was almost impossible to console him, and it was in vain to assure him that the attack had been produced by physical causes.

"Do you want to marry any one in particular?" I asked, at last, to divert his thoughts, if I could, from the present.

"No," said he; "at least, — of course she is out of the question, — only I thought perhaps some day I should have liked to have a wife and children and a home of my own. Why, the counting-house is not so dreary as this place sometimes seems to me."

And then, though it was indeed no time for love-confidences, I could not help asking him who it was that was out of the question.

Guy Griffiths shrugged his great round shoulders impatiently, and gave something between a groan and sigh, and a smile, dark and sulky as he looked at times, a smile brightened up his grim face very pleasantly.

"She don't even know my name," he said. "I saw her one night at the play, and then in a lane in the country a little time after. I found out who she was. She's a daughter of old Barly the stockbroker. Belinda, they call her, — Miss Belinda. It's rather a silly name, isn't it?" (This, of course, I politely denied.) "I'm sure I don't know what there is about her," he went on, in a gentle voice. "All the fellows down there were head over ears in love with her. I asked, — in fact I went down to Farmborough in hopes of meeting her again. I never saw such a sweet young creature, never. I never spoke to her in my life."

"But you know her father?" I asked.

"Old Barly?. Yes," said Guy. "His wife was my father's cousin, and we are each other's trustees for some money which was divided between me and Mrs. Barly. My parents never kept up with them much, but I was named trustee in my father's place when he died. I didn't like to refuse. I had never seen Belinda then. Do you like sweet, sleepy eyes that wake up now and then? Was that my mother calling?" For a minute he had forgotten the dreary present. It all came rushing back again. The bed creaked, the patient had moved a little on her pillow, and there was a gleam of some intelligence in her pinched face. The clock struck four in quick, tinkling tones; the rain seemed to have ceased, and the clouds to be parting; the rooms turned suddenly chill, though the fires were burning.

When I went home, about five o'clock, all the stars had come out and were shooting brilliantly overhead. The garden seemed full of a sudden freshness and of secret life stirring in the darkness; the sick woman's light was burning faintly, and in my own window the little bright lamp was flickering which H.'s kind fingers had trimmed and put there ready for me when I should return. When we reached the little gate Guy opened it and let me pass under some dripping green creeper which had been blown loose from the wall. He took my cold hand in both his big ones, and began to say something that ended in a sort of inarticulate sound, as he turned away and trudged back to his post again. I thought of the many meetings and partings at this little postern gate, and last words and protestations. Some may have been more sentimental, perhaps, than this one, but Guy's grunt of gratitude was more affecting to me than many a long string of words. I felt very sorry for him, poor old fellow, as I barred the door and climbed upstairs to my room. He sat up watching till the morning. But I was tired and soon went to sleep.

II.

SOME people do very well for a time Chances are propitious; the way lies straight before them up a gentle inclined plane, with a pleasant prospect on either side. They go rolling straight on, they don't exactly know how, and take it for granted that it is their own prudence and good driving and deserts which have brought them prosperously so far 'upon their journey. And then one day they come to a turnpike and destiny pops out of its little box and demands a toll, or prudence trips, or good sense shies at a scarecrow put up by the wayside, — or nobody knows why, but the whole machine breaks down on the road and can't be set going again. And then other vehicles go past it, hand-trucks, perambulators, cabs, omnibuses, and great, prosperous barouches, and the people who were sitting in the broken-down equipage get out and walk away on foot.

On that celebrated and melancholy Black Monday of which we have all heard, poor John Barly and his three daughters came down the carpeted steps of their comfortable sociable for the last time, and disappeared at the wicket of a little suburban cottage, — disappeared out of the prosperous, pompous, highly respectable circle in which they had gyrated, dragged about by two fat bay horses, in the greatest decorum and respectability; dining out, receiving their friends, returning their civilities. Miss Barlys had left large cards with their names engraved upon them in return for other large cards upon which were inscribed equally respectable names, and the addresses of other equally commodious family mansions. A mansion — so the house-agents tell us — is a house like another with the addition of a back staircase. The Barlys and all their friends had back staircases to their houses and to their daily life as well. They only wished to contemplate the broad, swept, carpeted drawing-room flights. Indeed, to Anna and Fanny Barly, this making the best of things, card-leaving and visiting, seemed a business of vital importance. The youngest of the girls, who had been christened by the pretty silly name of Belinda, had only lately come home from school, and did not value these splendors and proprieties so highly as her sisters did. She had no great love for the life they led. Sometimes looking over the balusters of their great house in Capulet Square, she had yawned out loud from very weariness, and then she would hear the sound echoing all the way up to the skylight and reverberating down from baluster to baluster. If she went into the drawing-room, instead of the yawning echoes the shrill voices of Anna and of Fanny were vibrating monotonously as they complimented Lady Ogden upon her new barouche, until Belinda could bear it no longer, and would jump up and run away to her bedroom to escape it all. She had a handsome bedroom, draped in green damask, becarpeted, four-posted, with an enormous mahogany wardrobe, of which poor Belle was dreadfully afraid, for the doors would fly open of their own accord in the dead of night, revealing dark abysses and depths unknown, with black ghosts hovering suspended or motionless and biding their time. There were other horrors: shrouds waving in the blackness, feet stirring, and low creakings of garroters, which she did not dare to dwell upon, as she hastily locked the doors and pushed the writing-table against them.

It must, therefore, be confessed, that to Belinda the days had been long and oppressive sometimes in this handsomely appointed Tyburnean palace. Anna, the eldest sister, was queen-regnant; she had both ability and inclination to take the lead. She was short, broad, and dignified, and some years older than either of her sisters. Her father respected her business-like mind, admired her ambition, regretted sometimes secretly that she had never been able to make up her mind to accept any of the eligible young junior partners, the doctor, the curate, who had severally proposed to her. But then, of course, as Anna often said, they could not possibly have got on without her at home. She had been in no hurry to leave the comfortable kingdom where she reigned in undisputed authority, ratifying the decisions of the ministry downstairs, appealed to by the butler, respectfully dreaded by both the housemaids. Who was there to go against her? Mr. Barly was in town all day and left everything to her; Fanny, the second sister, was her faithful ally. Fanny was sprightly, twenty-one, with black eyes, and a curl that was much admired. She was fond of fashion, flirting, and finery; inquisitive, talkative, feeble-minded, and entirely devoted to Anna. As for Belle, she had only come back from school the other day. Anna could not quite understand her at times. Fanny was of age and content to do as she was bid; here was Belle, at eighteen, asserting herself very strangely. Anna and Fanny seemed to pair off somehow, and Belle always had to hold her own without assistance, unless, indeed, her father was present. He had a great tenderness and affection for his youngest child, and the happiest hour of the day to Belinda was when she heard him come home and call for her in his cheerful, quavering voice. By degrees it seemed to her, as she listened, that the cheerfulness seemed to be dying out of his voice, and only the quaver remained; but that may have been fancy and because she had taken a childish dislike to the echoes in the house.

At dinner-time Anna used to ask her father how things were going in the City, and whether shirtings had risen any higher, and at what premium the Tre Rosas shares were held in the market. These were some shares in a Cornish mine company of which Mr. Barly was a director. Anna thought so highly of the whole concern that she had been anxious to invest a portion of her own and her sister Fanny's money in it. They had some small inheritance from their mother, of part of which they had the control when they came of age; the rest was invested in the Funds in Mr. Griffiths' name, and could not be touched. Poor Belle, being a minor, had to be content with sixty pounds a year for her pin-money, which was all she could get for her two thousand pounds.

When Anna talked business Mr. Barly used to be quite dazzled by her practical clear-headedness, her calm foresight, her powers of rapid calculation. Fanny used to prick up her ears and ask, shaking her curls playfully, how much girls must have to be heiresses, and did Anna think they should ever be heiresses? Anna would smile and nod her head, in a calm and chastened sort of way, at this childish impatience. "You should be very thankful, Frances, for all you have to look to, and for your excellent prospects. Emily Ogden, with all her fine airs, would not be sorry to be in your place."

At which Fanny blushed up bright red, and Belinda jumped impatiently upon her chair, blinking her white eyelids impatiently over her clear gray eyes, as she had a way of doing. "I can't bear talking about money," said she; "anything is better ...." Then she too stopped short and blushed.

"Papa," interrupted Fanny, playfully, "when will you escort us to the pantomime again? The Ogdens are all going next Tuesday, and you have been most naughty, and not taken us anywhere for such a long time."

Mr. Barly, who rarely refused anything anybody asked him, pushed his chair away from the table and answered, with strange impatience for him, — "My dear, I have had no time lately for plays and amusements of any sort. After working from morning to night for you all, I am tired, and want a little peace of an evening. I have neither spirits nor — "

"Dear papa," said Belinda, eagerly, "come up into the drawing-room and sit in the easy-chair, and let me play you to sleep."

As she spoke, Belinda smiled a delightful fresh, sweet, tender smile, like sunshine falling on a fair landscape. No wonder the little stockbroker was fond of his youngest daughter. Frances was pouting. Anna frowned slightly as she locked up the wine and turned over in her mind whether she might not write to the Ogdens and ask them to let Frances join their party. As for Belinda, playing Mozart to her father in the dim drawing-room upstairs, she was struck by the worn and harassed look in his face as he slept, snoring gently in accompaniment to her music. It was the last time Belle ever played upon the old piano.

Three or four days after, the crash came. The great Tre Rosas Mining Company (Limited) had failed, and the old-established house of Barly & Co. unexpectedly stopped payment.

If poor Mr. Barly had done it on purpose, his ruin could not have been more complete and ingenious. When his affairs came to be looked into, and his liabilities had been met, it was found that an immense fortune had been muddled away, and that scarcely anything would be left but a small furnished cottage, which had been given for her life to an old aunt just deceased, and which reverted to Fanny, her godchild, and the small sum which still remained in the three per cents., of which mention has been made, and which could not be touched until

Belle, the youngest of three daughters, should come of age.

After two or three miserable days of confusion, — during which the machine which had been set going·with so much. trouble still revolved once or twice with the force of its own impetus, the butler answering the bell, the footman bringing up the coals, the cook sending up the dinner as usual, — suddenly everything collapsed, and the great mass of furniture, servants, human creatures, animals, carriages, business and pleasure engagements, seemed overthrown together in a great struggling mass, panting and bewildered and trying to get free from the confusion of particles that no longer belonged to one another.

First the cook packed up her things and some nice damask table-cloths and napkins, a pair of sheets, and Miss Barly's umbrella, which happened to be hanging in the hall; then the three ladies drove off with their father to the cottage, where it was decided they should go to be out of the way of any unpleasantness. He had no heart to begin again, and was determined to give up the battle. Belle sat with her father on the back seat of the carriage, looking up into his haggard face a little wistfully, and trying to be as miserable as the others. She could not help it, — a cottage in the country, ruin, roses, novelty, clean chintzes instead of damask, a little room with mignonette, cocks crowing, had a wicked, morbid attraction for her which she could not overcome. She had longed for such a life when she had gone down to stay with the Ogdens at Farmborough last month, and had seen several haystacks and lovely little thatched cottages, where she had felt she would have liked to spend the rest of her days; one in particular had taken her fancy, with dear little latticed windows and a pigeon-cote, and two rosy little babies with a kitten toddling out from the ivy porch; but a great rough-looking man had come up in a slouched wide-awake and frightened Emily Ogden so much that she had pulled Belinda away in a hurry ... but here a sob from Fanny brought Belle back to her place in the barouche.

Anna felt that she must bear up, and nerved herself to the effort. Upon her the blow fell more heavily than upon any of the others. Indignant, injured, angry with her father, furious with the managers, the directors, the shareholders, the secretary, the unfortunate company, with the Bankruptcy Court, the Ogdens, the laws of fate, the world in general, with Fanny for sobbing, and with Belle for looking placid, she sat blankly staring out of the window as they drove past the houses where they had visited, and where she had been entertained an honored guest; and now — she put the hateful thought away — bankrupt, disgraced! Her bonnet was crushed in; she did not say a word; but her face looked quite fierce and old, and frightened Fanny into fresh lamentations. These hysterics had been first brought on by the sight of Emily Ogden driving by in the new barouche. This was quite too much for her poor friend's fortitude. "Emily will drop us, I know she will," sobbed Fanny. "O Anna! will they ever come and ask us to their Thursday luncheon-parties any more?" ·

"My children," said Mr. Barly, with a placid groan, pulling up the window, "we are disgraced; we can only hide our heads away from the world. Do not expect that any one will ever come near us again." At which announcement Fanny went off into new tears and bewailings. As for the kind, bewildered, weak-headed, soft-hearted little man, he had been so utterly worn out, harassed, worried, and wearied of late, that it was almost a relief to him to think that this was indeed the case. He sat holding Belle's hand in his, stroking and patting it, and wondering that people so near London did not keep the roads in better repair. "We must be getting near our new abode," said he at last almost cheerfully.

"You speak as if you were glad of our shame, papa," said Anna, suddenly, turning round upon him.

"Oh, hush!" cried Belle, indignantly. Fortunately the coachman stopped at this moment on a spot a very long way off from Capulet Square; and, leaning from his box, asked if it was that there little box across the common.

"Oh, what a sweet little place!" cried Belinda. But her heart rather sank as she told this dreadful story.

Myrtle Cottage was a melancholy little tumbledown place, looking over Dumbleton Common, which they had been crossing all this time. It was covered with stucco, cracked and stained and mouldy. There was a stained-glass window, which was broken. The veranda wanted painting. From outside it was evident that the white muslin curtains were not so fresh as they might have been. There was a little garden in front, planted with durable materials. Even out of doors, in the gardens in the

suburbs, the box-edges, the laurel-bushes, and the fusty old jessamines are apt to look shabby in time, if they are never renewed. A certain amount of time and money might, perhaps, have made Myrtle Cottage into a pleasant little habitation; but (judging from appearances) its last inhabitants seemed to have been in some want of both these commodities. Its helpless new occupants were not likely to have much of either to spare. A little dining-room, with glass drop candlesticks and a rickety table, and a print of a church and a dissenting minister on the wall. A little drawing-room, with a great horse-hair sofa, a huge round table in the middle of the room, and more glass drop candlesticks, also a small work-table of glass over faded worsted embroidery. Four little bedrooms, mousey, musty, snuffy, with four-posts as terrific as any they had left behind, and a small, black dungeon for a maid-servant. This was the little paradise which Belle had been picturing to herself all along the road, and at which she looked round half-sighing, half-dismayed. Their bundles, baskets, blankets were handed in, and a cart full of boxes had arrived. Fanny's parrot was shrieking at the top of its voice on the narrow landing.

"What fun!" cried Belinda, sturdily, instantly setting to work to get things into some order, while Fanny lay exhausted upon the horse-hair sofa; and Anna, in her haughtiest tones, desired the coachman to drive home, and stood watching the receding carriage until it had dwindled away into the distance, — coachman, hammer-cloth, bay horses, respectability, and all. When she re-entered the house, the parrot was screeching still, and Martha, the under-housemaid, — now transformed into a sort of extract of butler, footman, ladies'-maid, and cook, — was frying some sausages, of which the vulgar smell pervaded the place.

———

III.

Belle exclaimed, but it required all her courage and natural brightness of spirit to go on looking at the bright side of things, praising the cottage, working in the garden, giving secret assistance to the two bewildered maids who waited on the reduced little family, cheering her father, smiling, and putting the best face on things, as her sisters used to do at home. If it had been all front stairs in Capulet Square, it was all back staircase at the cottage. Rural roses, calm sunsets, long shadows across the common are all very well; but when puffs of smoke come out of the chimney and fill the little place; when, if the window is opened, a rush of wind and dust — worse than smoke — comes eddying into the room, and careers round the four narrow walls; when poor little Fanny coughs and shudders, and wraps her shawl more closely round her with a groan; when the smell of the kitchen frying-pan perfumes the house, and a mouse scampers out of the cupboard, and black beetles lie struggling in the milk-jugs, and the pump runs dry, and spiders crawl out of the tea-caddy, and so forth; then, indeed, Belle deserves some credit for being cheerful under difficulties. She could not pretend to very high spirits, but she was brisk and willing, and ready to smile at her father's little occasional puns and feeble attempts at jocularity. Anna, who had been so admirable as a general, broke down under the fatigue of the actual labor in the trenches which belonged to their new life. A great many people can order others about very brilliantly and satisfactorily, who fail when they have to do the work themselves.

Some of the neighbors called upon them, but the Ogdens never appeared. Poor little Fanny used to take her lace-work, and sit stitching and looping her thread at the window which overlooked the common and its broad roads, crossing and recrossing the plain; carriages came rolling along, people came walking, children ran past the windows of the little cottage; but the Ogdens never. Once Fanny thought she recognized the barouche, — Lady Ogden and Emily sitting in front, Matthew Ogden on the back seat; surely, yes, surely it was him. But the carriage rolled off in a cloud of dust, and disappeared behind the wall of the neighboring park; and Frances finished the loop, and passed her needle in and out of the muslin, feeling as if it was through her poor little heart that she was piercing and sticking; she pulled out a long thread, and it seemed to her as if the sunset stained it red like blood.

In the mean while, Belle's voice had been singing away overhead, and Fanny, going upstairs presently, found her, with one of the maids, clearing out one of the upper rooms. The window was open, the furniture was piled up in the middle. Belle, with her sleeves tucked up, and her dress carefully pinned out of the dust, was standing on a chair, hammer in hand, and fixing up

some dimity curtains against the window. Table-cloths, brooms, pails and brushes were lying about, and everything looked in perfect confusion. As Fanny stood looking and exclaiming, Anna also came to the door from her own room, where she had been taking a melancholy nap.

"What a mess you are making here!" cried the elder sister, very angrily. How can you take up Martha's time, Belinda? And oh! how can you forget yourself to this degree? You seem to exult in your father's disgrace." Belinda flushed up.

"Really, Anna, I do not know what you mean," said she, turning round, vexed for a minute, and clasping a long curtain in both arms. "I could not bear to see my father's room looking so shabby and neglected; there is no disgrace in attending to his comfort. See, we have taken down those dusty curtains, and we are going to put up some others," said the girl, springing down from the chair and exhibiting her treasures.

"And pray where is the money to come from," said Anna, "to pay for these wonderful changes?"

"They cost no money," said Belinda, laughing. "I made them myself with my own two hands. Don't you remember my old white dress that you never liked, Anna? Look how I have pricked my finger. Now, go down," said the girl, in her pretty, imperative way, "and don't come up again till I call you."

Go down at Belle's bidding. . . . .

Anna went off fuming, and immediately set to work also, but in a different fashion. She unfortunately found that her father had returned, and was sitting in the little sitting-room down below by himself, with a limp paper of the day before him open upon his knees. He was not reading. He seemed out of spirits, and was gazing in a melancholy way at the smouldering fire, and rubbing his bald head in a perplexed and troubled manner. Seeing this, the silly woman, by way of cheering and comforting the poor old man, began to exclaim at Belinda's behavior, to irritate him, and overwhelm him with allusions and reproaches.

"Scrubbing and slaving with her own hands," said Anna. "Forgetting herself; bringing us down lower indeed than we are already sunk. Papa, she will not listen to me. You should tell her that you forbid her to put us all to shame by her behavior."

When Belle, panting, weary, triumphant,

2

and with a blackened nose and rosy cheek, opened the door of the room presently, and called her father exultingly, she did not notice, as she ran upstairs before him, how wearily he followed her. A flood of light came from the dreary little room overhead. It had been transformed into a bower of white dimity, bright windows, clean muslin blinds. The fusty old carpet was gone, and a clean crumb-cloth had been put down, with a comfortable rug before the fireplace. A nosegay of jessamine stood on the chimney, and at each corner of the four-post bed, the absurd young decorator had stuck a smart bow, made out of some of her own blue ribbons, in place of the terrible plumes and tassels which had waved there in dust and darkness before. One of the two arm-chairs which blocked up the wall of the dining-room had been also covered out of some of Belinda's stores, and stood comfortably near the open window. The sun was setting over the great common outside, behind the mill and the distant fringe of elm-trees. Martha, standing all illuminated by the sunshine, with her mop in her hand, was grinning from ear to ear, and Belle turned and rushed into her father's arms. But Mr. Barly was quite overcome.

"My child," he said, "why do you trouble yourself so much for me? Your sister has told me all. I don't deserve it. I cannot bear that you should be brought to this. My Belle working and slaving with your own hands through my fault, — through my fault."

The old man sat down on the side of the bed by which he had been standing, and laid his face in his hands, in a perfect agony of remorse and regret. Belinda was dismayed by the result of her labors. In vain she tried to cheer him and comfort him. The sweeter she seemed in his eyes, the more miserable the poor father grew at the condition to which he had brought her.

For many days after he went about in a sort of despair, thinking what he could do to retrieve his ruined fortunes, and if Belinda still rose betimes to see to his comfort and the better ordering of the confused little household, she took care not to let it be known. Anna came down at nine, Fanny at ten. Anna would then spend several hours regretting her former dignities, reading the newspaper and the fashionable intelligence, while the dismal strains of Fanny's piano (there was a jangling piano in the little drawing-room) streamed across the common. To a stormy spring, with wind flying, and dust dashing against the window-panes, and gray clouds swiftly bearing across the wide, open country, had succeeded a warm and brilliant summer, with sunshine flooding and spreading over the country. Anna and Fanny were able to get out a little now, but they were soon tired, and would sit down under a tree and remark to one another how greatly they missed their accustomed drives. Belinda, who had sometimes at first disappeared now and then to cry mysteriously a little bit by herself over her troubles, now discovered that at eighteen, with good health and plenty to do, happiness is possible, even without a carriage.

One day Mr. Barly, who still went into the city from habit, came home with some news which had greatly excited him. Wheal Tre Rosas, of which he still held a great many shares, which he had never been able to dispose of, had been giving some signs of life. A fresh call was to be made: some capitalist, with more money than he evidently knew what to do with, had been buying up a great deal of the stock. The works were to be resumed. Mr. Barly had always been satisfied that the concern was a good one. He would give everything he had, he told Anna that evening, to be able to raise enough money now to buy up more of the shares. His fortune was made if he could do so; his children replaced in their proper position, and his name restored. Anna was in a state of greater flutter, if possible, than her father himself. Belle sighed; she could not help feeling doubtful, but she did not like to say much on the subject.

"Papa, this Wheal has proved a very treacherous wheel of fortune. to us," she hazarded, blushing, and bending over her sewing; "we are very, very happy as we are."

"Happy?" said Anna, with a sneer.

"Really, Belinda, you are too romantic," said Fanny, with a titter; while Mr. Barly cried out, in an excited way, "that she should be happier yet, and all her goodness and dutifulness should be rewarded in time." A sort of presentiment of evil came over Belinda, and her eyes filled up with tears; but she stitched them away and said no more.

Unfortunately the only money Mr. Barly could think of to lay his hands upon was that sum in the three per cents. upon which they were now living; and even if he chose he could not touch any of it, until Belinda came of age; unless, indeed, young Mr.

Griffiths would give him permission to do so.

"Go to him, papa," cried Anna, enthusiastically. "Go to him; entreat, insist upon it, if necessary."

All that evening Anna and Frances talked over their brilliant prospects.

"I should like to see the Ogdens again," said poor little Fanny.

"Perhaps we shall if we go back to Capulet Square."

"Certainly, certainly," said Anna.

"I have heard that this Mr. Griffiths is a most uncouth and uncivilized person to deal with," continued Miss Barly, with her finger on her chin. "Papa, wouldn't it be better for me to go to Mr. Griffiths instead of you?" This, however, Mr. Barly would not consent to.

Anna could hardly contain her vexation and spite when he came back next day dispirited, crestfallen, and utterly wretched and disappointed. Mr. Griffiths would have nothing to say to it.

"What's the good of a trustee," said he to Mr. Barly, "if he were to let you invest your money in such a speculative chance as that? Take my advice, and sell out your shares now, if you can, for anything you can get."

"A surly, disagreeable fellow," said poor old Mr. Barly. "I heartily wish he had nothing to do with our affairs."

Anna fairly stamped with rage. "What insolence, when it is our own! Papa, you have no spirit to allow such interference."

Mr. Barly looked at her gravely, and said he should not allow it. Anna did not know what he meant.

Belinda was not easy about her father all this time. He came and went in an odd, excited sort of way, stopping short sometimes as he was walking across the room, and standing absorbed in thought. One day he went into the city unexpectedly about the middle of the day, and came back looking quite odd, pale, with curious eyes; something was wrong, she could not tell what. In the mean time Wheal Tre Rosas seemed, spite of Mr. Griffiths' prophecies, to be steadily rising in the world. More business had been done; the shares were a trifle higher. A meeting of directors was convened, and actually a small dividend was declared at midsummer. It really seemed as if there was some chance after all that Anna should be reinstated in the barouche, in Capulet Square, and her place in society. She and Fanny were half wild with delight.

"When we leave," — was the beginning of every sentence they uttered. Fanny wrote the good news to her friend Miss Ogden, and, under these circumstances, to Fanny's unfeigned delight, Emily Ogden thought herself justified in driving over to the village one fine afternoon and affably partaking of a cracked cupful of five o'clock tea. It was slightly smoked, and the milk was turned. Belinda had gone out for a walk and was not there to see to it all; I am afraid she did not quite forgive Emily the part she had played, and could not make up her mind to meet her.

One morning Anna was much excited by the arrival of a letter directed to Mr. Barly in great round handwriting, and with a huge seal, all over bears and griffins. Her father was forever expecting news of his beloved Tre Rosas, and he broke the seal with some curiosity. But this was only an invitation to dine and sleep at Castle Gardens from Mr. Griffiths, who said he had an offer to make Mr. Barly, and concluded by saying that he hoped Mr. Barly forgave him for the ungracious part he had been obliged to play the other day, and that, in like circumstances, he would do the same by him.

"I shan't go," said Mr. Burly, a little doggedly, putting the letter down.

"Not go, papa! Why, you my be able to talk him over if you get him quietly to yourself. Certainly you must go, papa," said Anna. "Oh! I'm sure he means to relent. How nice!" said Fanny. Even Belinda thought it was a pity he should not accept the invitation, and Mr. Burly gave way as usual. He asked them if they had any commands for him in town.

"Oh, thank you, papa," said Frances. "If you are going shopping, I wish you would bring me back a blue alpaca, and a white grenadine, and a pink sou-poult, and a — "

"My dear Fanny, that will be quite sufficient for the short time you remain here," interrupted Anna, who went on to give her father several commissions of her own, — some writing-paper stamped with Barly Lodge and their crest in one corner; a jacket with buttons for the knife-boy they had lately engaged upon the strength of their coming good fortune; a new umbrella, house-agent's list of mansions in the neighborhood of Capulet Square, the *Journal des Modes*, and the *New Court Guide*. "Let me see, there was something else," said Anna.

"Belle," said Mr. Barly, "how comes it

you ask for nothing? What can I bring you, my child?"

Belle looked up with one of her bright, melancholy smiles, and replied, "If you should see any roses, papa, I think I should like a bunch of roses. We have none in the garden."

"Roses!" cried Fanny, laughing. "I didn't know you cared for anything but what was useful, Belle."

"I quite expected you would ask for a saucepan, or a mustard-pot," said Anna, with a sneer.

Belle sighed again, and then the three went and stood at the garden-gate to see their father off. It made a pretty little group for the geese on the common to contemplate, — the two young sisters at the wicket, the elder under the shade of the veranda, Belle upright, smiling, waving her slim hand; she was above the middle height, she had fair hair and dark eyebrows and gray eyes, over which she had a peculiar way of blinking her smooth white eyelids; — and all about, the birds, the soft winds, the great green common with its gorgeous furze-blossom blazing against the low bank of clouds in the horizon. Close at hand a white pony was tranquilly cropping the grass, and two little village children were standing outside the railings, gazing up open-mouthed at the pretty ladies who lived at the cottage.

————

IV.

THE clouds which had been gathering all the afternoon broke shortly before Mr. Barly reached his entertainer's house. He had tried to get there through Kensington Gardens, but could not make out the way, and went wandering round and round in some perplexity under the great trees with their creaking branches. The storm did not last long, and the clouds dispersed at sunset. When Mr. Barly rang at the gate of the villa in Castle Gardens at last that evening he was weary, wet through, and far less triumphant than he had been when he left home in the morning. The butler who let him in gave the bag which he had been carrying to the footman and showed him the way upstairs immediately, to the comfortable room which had been made ready for him. Upholsterers had done the work on the whole better than Belle with all her loving labor. The chairs were softer than her print-covered horse-hair cushions. The wax-lights were burning although it was broad daylight. Mr. Barly went to the bay-window. The garden outside was a sight to see: smooth lawns, arches, roses in profusion and abundance, hanging and climbing and clustering everywhere, a distant gleam of a fountain, of a golden sky, a chirruping and rustling in the bushes and trellises after the storm. The sunset which was lighting up the fern on the rain-sprinkled common was twinkling through the rose-petals here, bringing out odors and aromas and whiffs of delicious scent. Mr. Barly thought of Belle, and how he should like to see her flitting about in the garden and picking roses to her heart's content. As he stood there he thought too with a pang of his wife whom he had lost, and sighed in a sort of despair at the troubles which had fallen upon him of late. What would he not give to undo the work of the last few months, he thought — nay, of the last few days? He had once come to this very house with his wife in their early days of marriage. He remembered it now, although he had not thought of it before.

Sometimes it happens to us all that things which happened ever so long ago seem to make a start out of their proper places in the course of time, and come after us, until they catch us up, as it were, and surround us, so that one can hear the voices, and see the faces and colors, and feel the old sensations and thrills as keenly as at the time they occurred, — all so curiously and strangely vivid that one can scarcely conceive it possible that years and years perhaps have passed since it all happened, and that their present shock proceeds from ancient and almost forgotten impulse. And so, as Mr. Barly looked and remembered and thought of the past, a sudden remorse and shame came over him. He seemed to see his wife standing in the garden, holding the roses up over her head, looking like Belle, — like, yet unlike. Why it should have been so, at the thought of his wife among the flowers, I cannot tell; but as he remembered her he began to think of what he had done, — that he was there in the house of the man he had defrauded, — he began to ask himself how could he face him? how could he sit down beside him at table, and break his bread? The poor old fellow fell back with a groan in one of the comfortable armchairs. Should he confess? Oh, no — no, that would be the most terrible of all!

What he had done is simply told. When

Guy Griffiths refused to let Mr. Barly lay hands on any of the money which he had in trust for his daughters, the foolish and angry old man had sold out a portion of the sum belonging to Mr. Griffiths which still remained in his own name. It had not seemed like dishonesty at the time, but now he would have gladly — oh, how gladly! — awakened to find it all a dream. He dressed mechanically, turning over every possible chance in his own mind. Let Wheal Tre Rosas go on and prosper, the first money should go to repay his loan, and no one should be the wiser. He went down into the library again when he was ready. It was empty still, and, to his relief, the master of the house had not yet come back. He waited a very long time, looking at the clock, at the reviews on the table, at the picture of Mrs. Griffiths, whom he could remember in her youth, upon the wall. The butler came in again to say that his master had not yet returned. Some message had come by a boy, which was not very intelligible, — he had been detained in the city. Mrs. Griffiths was not well enough to leave her room, but she hoped Mr. Barly would order dinner, — anything he required, — and that her son would shortly return.

It was very late. There was nothing else to be done. Mr. Barly found a fire lighted in the great dining-room, dinner laid, one plate and one knife and fork, at the end of the long table. The dinner was excellent, — so was the wine. The butler uncorked a bottle of champagne, the cook sent up chickens and all sorts of good things. Mr. Barly almost felt as if he, by some strange metempsychosis, had been converted into the owner of this handsome dwelling, and all that belonged to it. At twelve o'clock Mr. Griffiths had not yet returned, and his guest, after a somewhat perplexed and solitary meal, retired to rest.

Mr. Barly breakfasted by himself again next morning. Mr. Griffiths had not returned all night. In his secret heart Mr. Griffiths' guest was almost relieved by the absence of his entertainer; it seemed like a respite. Perhaps, after all, everything would go well, and the confession, which he had contemplated with such terror the night before, need never be made. For the present, it was clearly no use to wait any longer at the house. Mr. Barly asked for a cab to take him to the station, left his compliments and regrets and a small sum of money behind him, and then, as the cab delayed,

strolled out into the front garden to wait for it.

Even in the front court the roses were all abloom; a great snow-cluster was growing over the doorway, a pretty tea-rose was hanging its head over the scraper; against the outer railing which separated the house from the road rose-trees had been planted. The beautiful pink fragrant heads were pushing through the iron railings, and a delicious little rose-wind come blowing in the poor old fellow's face. He began to think — no wonder — of Belle and her fancy for roses, and mechanically, without much reflecting upon what he was about, he stopped and inhaled the ravishing sweet smell of the great dewy flowers, and then put out his hand and gathered one; and as he gathered it a sharp thorn ran into his finger, and a heavy grasp was laid upon his shoulder. . . . . .

"So it is you, is it, who sneak in and steal my roses?" said an angry voice. "Now that I know who it is, I shall give you in charge."

Mr. Barly looked round greatly startled. He met the fierce glare of two dark-brown eyes under shaggy brows that were frowning very fiercely. A broad, thick-set, round-shouldered young man of forbidding aspect had laid hold of him. The young man let go his grasp when he saw the mistake he had made, but did not cease frowning.

"Oh! it is you, Mr. Barly," he said.

"I was just going," said the stockbroker, meekly. "I am glad you have returned in time for me to see you, Mr. Griffiths. I am sorry I took your rose. My youngest daughter is fond of them, and I thought I might, out of all this gardenful, — you would not — she had asked —"

There was something so stern and unforgiving in Mr. Griffiths' face that the merchant stumbled in his words, and stopped short, surprised, in the midst of his explanations.

"The roses were not yours, not if there were ten gardens full. I won't have my roses broken off," said Griffiths; "they should be cut with a knife. Come back with me; I want to have a little talk with you, Mr. Barly."

Somehow the old fellow's heart began to beat, and he felt himself turn rather sick.

"I was detained last night by some trouble in my office. One of my clerks in whom I thought I could have trusted, absconded yesterday afternoon. I have been all the way to Liverpool in pursuit of him.

What do you think should be done with him?" And Mr. Griffiths, from under his thick eyebrows, gave a quick glance at his present victim, and seemed to expect some sort of answer.

"You prosperous men 'cannot realize what it is to be greatly tempted," said Mr. Barly, with a faint smile.

"Do you know that Wheal Tre Rosas has come to grief a second time?" said young Mr. Griffiths, abruptly, holding out the morning's *Times*, as they walked along. "I am *not* a prosperous man; I had a great many shares in that unlucky concern."

Poor Barly stopped short and turned quite pale, and began to shake so that he had to put his hand out and lean against the wall. Failed! Was he doomed to misfortune? Then there was never any chance for him,—never. No hope! No hope of paying back the debt which weighed upon his conscience. He could not realize it. Failed! The rose had fallen to the ground; the poor unlucky man stood still, staring blankly in the other's grim, unrelenting face. "I am ruined," he said.

"You are ruined! Is that the worst you, have to tell me?" said Mr. Griffiths, still looking piercingly at him. Then the other felt that he knew all.

"I have been very unfortunate—and very much to blame," said Mr. Barly, still trembling;—"terribly to blame, Mr. Griffiths. I can only throw myself upon your clemency."

"My clemency! my mercy! I am no philanthropist," said Guy, savagely. "I am a man of business, and you have defrauded me!"

"Sir," said the stockbroker, finding some odd comfort in braving the worst, "you refused to let me take what was my own; I have sold out some of your money to invest in this' fatal concern. Heaven knows it was not for myself, but for the sake of—of—others; and I thought to repay you ere long. You can repay yourself now. You need not reproach me any more. You can send me to prison if you like. I—I—don't much care what happens. My Belle, my poor Belle,—my poor girls!"

All this time Guy said never a word. He motioned Mr. Barly to follow him into the library. Mr. Barly obeyed, and stood meekly waiting for the coming onslaught. He stood in the full glare of the morning sun, which was pouring through the unblinded window. His poor old scanty head was bent, and his hair stood on end in the sunshine.

His eyes, avoiding the glare, went vacantly travelling along the scroll-work on the fender, and so to the coal-scuttle and to the skirting on the wall, and back again. Dishonored,—yes. Bankrupt,—yes. Three-score years had brought him to this,—to shame, to trouble. It was a hard world for unlucky people; but Mr. Barly was too much broken, too weary and indifferent, to feel very bitterly even against the world. Meanwhile, Guy was going on with his reflections, and like those amongst us who are still young and strong, he could put more life and energy into his condemnation and judgment of actions done, than the unlucky perpetrators had to give to the very deeds themselves. Some folks do wrong as well as right, with scarcely more than half a mind to it.

"How could you do such a thing?" cried the young man, indignantly, beginning to rush up and down the room in his hasty, clumsy way, knocking against tables and chairs as he went along. "How could you do it?" he repeated. "I learned it yesterday, by chance. What can I say to you that your own conscience should not have told you already? How could you do it?"

Guy had reached the great end window, and stamped with vexation and a mixture of anger and sorrow. For all his fierceness and gruffness, he was sorry for the poor feeble old man, whose fate he held in his hand. There was the garden outside, and its treasure and glory of roses; there was the rose, lying on the ground, that old Barly had taken. It was lying broken and shining upon the gravel,—one rose out of the hundreds that were bursting, and blooming, and fainting and falling on their spreading stems. It was like the wrong old Barly had done his kinsman,—one little wrong Guy thought, one little handful out of all his abundance. He looked back, and by chance caught sight of their two figures reflected in the glass at the other end of the room,—his own image, the strong, round-backed, broad-shouldered young man, with gleaming white teeth and black bristling hair; the feeble and uncertain culprit, with his broken, wandering looks, waiting his sentence. It was not Guy who delivered it. It came,—no very terrible one after all,—prompted by some unaccountable secret voice and impulse. Have we not all of us sometimes suddenly felt ashamed in our lives in the face of misfortune and sorrow? Are we Pharisees, standing in the market-place, with our phylacteries displayed to the world? We ask ourselves, in dismay, does this man go home justified rather than we? Guy was not the less worthy of his Belinda, poor fellow, because a thought of her crossed his mind, and because he blushed up, and a gentle look came into his eyes, and a shame into his heart, — a shame of his strength and prosperousness, of his probity and high honor. When had he been tempted? What was it but a chance that he had been born what he was? And yet old Barly, in all his troubles, had a treasure in his possession for which Guy felt he would give all his good fortune and good repute, his roses, — red, white, and golden, — his best heart's devotion, which he secretly felt to be worth all the rest. Now was the time, the young man thought, to make that proposition which he had in his mind.

"Look here," said Guy, hanging his great shaggy head, and speaking quickly and thickly, as if he was the culprit instead of the accuser. "You imply it was for your daughter's sake that you cheated me. I cannot consent to act as you would have me do, and take your daughter's money to pay myself back. But if one of them, — Miss Belinda, since she likes roses, — chooses to come here and work the debt off, she can do so. My mother is in bad health, and wants a companion; she will engage her at — let me see — a hundred guineas a year, and in this way, by degrees, the debt will be cleared off."

"In twenty years!" said Mr. Barly, bewildered, relieved, astonished.

"Yes, in twenty years," said Guy, as if that was the most natural thing in the world. "Go home and consult her, and come back and give me the answer."

And as he spoke, the butler came in to say that the hansom was at the door.

Poor old Barly bent his worn, meek head and went out. He was shaken and utterly puzzled. If Guy had told him to climb up the chimney he would have obeyed. He could only do as he was bid. As it was, he clambered with difficulty into the hansom, told the man to go to the station for Dumbleton, and he was driving off gladly when some one called after the cab. The old man peered out anxiously. Had Griffiths changed his mind? Was his heart hardened like Pharaoh's at the eleventh hour?

It was certainly Guy who came hastily after the cab, looking more awkward and sulky than ever. "Hoy! Stop! You have forgotten the roses for your daughter," said he, thrusting in a great bunch of sweet foam and freshness. As the cab drove along, people passing by looked up and envied the man who was carrying such loveliness through the black and dreary London streets. Could they have seen the face looking out behind the roses they might have ceased to envy.

Belle was on the watch for her father at the garden-gate, and exclaimed with delight, as she saw him toiling up the hill from the station with his huge bunch of flowers. She came running to meet him with fluttering skirts and outstretched hands, and sweet smiles gladdening her face. "O papa, how lovely! Have you had a pleasant time?" Her father hardly responded. "Take the roses, Belle," he said. "I have paid for them dearly enough." He went into the house wearily, and sat down in the shabby arm-chair. And then he turned and called Belinda to him wistfully and put his trembling arm round about her. Poor old Barly was no mighty Jephthah; but his feeble old head bent with some such pathetic longing and remorse over his Belle as he drew her to him, and told her, in a few simple, broken words, all the story of what had befallen him in those few hours since he went away. He could not part from her. "I can't, I can't," he said, as the girl put her tender arms round his neck. . . . . .

Guy came to see me a few days after his interview with old Mr. Barly, and told me that his mother had surprised him by her willing acquiescence in the scheme. I could have explained matters to him a little, but I thought it best to say nothing. Mrs. Griffiths had overheard and understood a word or two of what he had said to me that night, when she was taken ill. Was it some sudden remorse for the past? Was it a new-born mother's tenderness stirring in her cold heart, which made her question and cross-question me the next time that I was alone with her? There had often been a talk of some companion or better sort of attendant. When the news came of poor old Barly's failure, it was Mrs. Griffiths herself who first vaguely alluded again to this scheme.

"I might engage one of those girls — the — the — Belinda, I think you called her?"

I was touched, and took her cold hand and kissed it.

"I am sure she would be an immense comfort to you," I said. "You would never regret your kindness."

The sick woman sighed and turned away impatiently, and the result was the invitation to dinner, which turned out so disastrously.

V.

WHEN Mr. Barly came down to breakfast, the morning after his return, he found another of those great, square, official-looking letters upon the table. There was a check in it for 100*l*. " You will have to meet heavy expenses," the young man wrote. " I am not sorry to have an opportunity of proving to you that it was not the money which you have taken from me I grudged, but the manner in which you took it. The only reparation you can make me is by keeping the enclosed for your present necessity."

In truth the family prospects were not very brilliant. Myrtle Cottage was resplendent with clean windows and well-scrubbed door-steps, but the furniture wanted repairing, the larder refilling. Belle could not darn up the broken flap of the dining-room table, nor conjure legs of mutton out of bare bones, though she got up ever so early; sweeping would not mend the hole in the carpet, nor could she dust the mildew-stains off the walls, the cracks out of the looking-glass.

Anna was morose, helpless, and jealous of the younger girl's influence over her father. Fanny was delicate; one gleam of happiness, however, streaked her horizon; Emily Ogden had written to invite her to spend a few days there. When Mr. Barly and his daughter had talked over Mr. Griffiths' proposition, Belle's own good sense told her that it would be folly to throw away this good chance. Let Mrs. Griffiths be ever so trying and difficult to deal with, and her son a thousand times sterner and ruder than he had already shown himself, she was determined to bear it all. Belinda knew her own powers, and felt as if she could endure anything, and that she should never forget the generosity and forbearance he had shown her poor father. Anna was delighted that her sister should go; she threw off the shawl in which she had muffled herself up ever since their reverses, brightened up wonderfully, talked mysteriously of Fanny's prospects as she helped both the girls to pack, made believe to shed a few tears as Belinda set off, and bustled back into the house with renewed importance. Belinda looked back and waved her hand,

but Anna's back was already turned upon her.

Poor Belinda! For all her courage and cheerfulness her heart sank a little as they reached the great bronze gates in Castle Gardens. She would have been more unhappy still if she had not had to keep up her father's spirits. It was almost dinner-time, and Mrs. Griffiths' maid came down with a message. Her mistress was tired, and just going to bed, and would see her in the morning; Mr. Griffiths was dining in town; Miss Williamson would call upon Miss Barly that evening.

Dinner had been laid as usual in the great dining-room, with its marble columns and draperies, and Dutch pictures of game and of birds and flowers. Three servants were in waiting, a great silver chandelier lighted the dismal meal, huge dish-covers were upheaved, decanters of wine were handed round, all the *entrées* and delicacies came over again. Belle tried to eat to keep her father in company. She even made little jokes, and whispered to him that they evidently meant to fatten her up. The poor old fellow cheered up by degrees; the good claret warmed his feeble pulse; the good fare comforted and strengthened him. " I wish Martha would make us ice puddings," said Belle, helping him to a glittering mass of pale-colored cream, with nutmeg and vanilla, and all sorts of delicious spices. He had just finished the last mouthful when the butler started and rushed out of the room, a door banged, a bell rang violently, a loud scraping was heard in the hall, and an echoing voice said, " Are they come? Are they in the dining-room?" And the crimson curtain was lifted up, and the master of the house entered the room carrying a bag and a great-coat over his arm. As he passed the sideboard the button of the coat caught in the fringe of a cloth which was spread upon it, and in a minute the cloth and all the glasses and plates which had been left there came to the ground with a wild crash, which would have made Belle laugh, if she had not been too nervous even to smile.

Guy merely told the servants to pick it all up, and put down the things he was carrying and walked straight across the room to the two frightened people at the end of the table. Poor fellow! After shaking hands with old Barly and giving his daughter an abrupt little nod, all he could find to say was, —

" I hope you came of your own free will,

Miss Barly?" and as he spoke he gave a shy scowl and eyed her all over.

"Yes," Belle answered, blinking her soft eyes to see him more clearly.

"Then I'm very much obliged to you," said Guy.

This was such an astonishingly civil answer that Belinda's courage rose.

Poor Belinda's heart failed her again when Griffiths, still in an agony of shyness, then turned to her father, and in his roughest voice said, —

"You leave early in the morning, but I hope we shall keep your daughter for a very long time."

Poor fellow! he meant no harm and only intended this by way of conversation. Belle in her secret heart said to herself that he was a cruel brute; and poor Guy, having made this impression, broken a dozen wineglasses, and gone through untold struggles of shyness, now wished them both goodnight.

"Good-night, Mr. Barly; good-night, Miss Belle," said he. Something in his voice caused Belle to relent a little.

"Good-night, Mr. Griffiths," said the girl, standing up, a slight, graceful figure, simple and nymph-like, amidst all this pomp of circumstance. As Griffiths shuffled out of the room he saw her still; all night he saw her in his dreams. That bright, winsome young creature dressed in white, soft folds, with all the gorgeous gildings and draperies, and the lights burning, and the pictures and gold cups glimmering round about her. They were his, and as many more of them as he chose; the inanimate, costly, sickening pomps and possessions; but a pure spirit like that, to be a bright, living companion for him? Ah, no! that was not to be, — not for him, not for such as him. Guy, for the first time in his life, as he went downstairs next morning, stopped and looked at himself attentively in the great glass on the staircase. He saw a great loutish, round-backed fellow, with a shaggy head and brown glittering eyes, and little strong, white teeth like a dog's; he gave an uncouth sudden caper of rage and regret at his own appearance. "To think that happiness and life itself and love eternal depend upon tailors and hair-oil," groaned poor Guy, as he went down to his room to write letters.

Mrs. Griffiths had not seen Belle the night before; she was always nervously averse to seeing strangers, but she had sent for me that evening, and as I was leav-

ing she asked me to go down and speak to Miss Barly before I went. Belinda was already in her room, but I ventured to knock at the door. She came to meet me with a bright, puzzled face and all her pretty hair falling loose about her face. She had not a notion who I was, but begged me to come in. When I had explained things a little, she pulled out a chair for me to sit down.

"This house seems to me so mysterious and unlike anything else I have ever known," said she, "that I'm very grateful to any one who will tell me what I'm to do here. Please sit down a little while."

I told her that she would have to write notes, to add up bills, to read to Mrs. Griffiths, and to come to me whenever she wanted any help or comfort. "You were quite right to come," said I. "They are excellent people. Guy is the kindest, best fellow in the whole world, and I have long heard of you, Miss Barly, and I'm sure such a good daughter as you have been will be rewarded some day."

Belle looked puzzled, grateful, a little proud, and very charming. She told me afterwards that it had been a great comfort to her father to hear of my little visit to her, and that she had succeeded in getting him away without any very painful scene.

Poor Belle! I wonder how many tears she shed that day after her father was gone? While she was waiting to be let in to Mrs. Griffiths she amused herself by wandering about the house, dropping a little tear here and there as she went along, and trying to think that it amused her to see so many yards of damask and staircarpeting, all exactly alike, so many acres of chintz of the same pattern.

"Mr. Griffiths desired me to say that this tower room was to be made ready for you to sit in, ma'am," said the respectful butler, meeting her and opening a door. "It has not been used before." And he gave her the key, to which a label was affixed, with "MISS BARLY'S ROOM" written upon it, in the house-keeper's scrawling handwriting.

Belle gave a little shriek of admiration. It was a square room, with four windows, overlooking the gardens, the distant park, and the broad, cheerful road which ran past the house. An ivy screen had been trained over one of the windows, roses were clustering in garlands round the deep, sill casements. There was an Indian carpet, and pretty silk curtains, and comfortable chintz chairs and sofas, upon which beautiful birds were flying and lilies wreathing. There was an old-fashioned-looking piano, too, and a great bookcase filled with books and music. "They certainly treat me in the most magnificent way," thought Belle, sinking down upon the sofa in the window which overlooked the rose-garden, and inhaling a delicious breath of fragrant air. "They can't mean to be very unkind." Belle, who was a little curious, it must be confessed, looked at everything, made secret notes in her mind, read the titles of the books, examined the china, discovered a balcony to her turret. There was a little writing-table, too, with paper and pens and inks of various colors, which especially pleased her. A glass cup of cut roses had been placed upon it, and two dear little green books, in one of which some one had left a paper-cutter.

The first was a book of fairy tales, from which I hope the good fairy editress will forgive me for stealing a sentence or two.

The other little green book was called the *Golden Treasury;* and when Belle took it up, it opened where the paper-cutter had been left, at the seventh page, and some one had scored the sonnet there. Belle read it, and somehow, as she read, the tears in her eyes started afresh.

"Being your slave, what should I do but tend
   Upon the hours and times of your desire?"

it began. "To ——" had been scrawled underneath; and then the letter following the "To" erased. Belle blinked her eyes over it, but could make nothing out. A little further on she found another scoring, —

"Oh, my love's like a red, red rose
   That's newly sprung in June!
Oh, my love's like the melody
   That's sweetly played in tune!"

and this was signed with a G.

"Love! That is not for me; but I wish I had a slave," thought poor Belle, hanging her head over the book as it lay open in her lap, "and that he was clever enough to tell me what my father is doing at this minute." She could imagine it for herself, alas! without any magic interference. She could see the dreary little cottage, her poor old father wearily returning alone. She nearly broke down at the thought, but some one knocked at the door at that instant, and she forced herself to be calm as one of the servants came in with a telegram. Belinda tore open her telegram in some alarm and trembling terror of bad news from home; and

then smiled a sweet, loving smile of relief. The telegram came from Guy. It was dated from his office. ("Your father desires me to send word that he is safe home. He sends his love. I have been to D. on business, and travelled down with him."

Belinda could not help saying to herself that Mr. Griffiths was very kind to have thought of her. His kindness gave her courage to meet his mother.

It was not very much that she had to do; but whatever it was she accomplished well and thoroughly, as was her way. Whatever the girl put her hand to she put her whole heart to at the same time. Her energy, sweetness, and good spirits cheered the sick woman and did her infinite good. Mrs. Griffiths took a great fancy to her, and liked to have her about her. Belle lunched with her the first day. She had better dine down below, Mrs. Griffiths said; and when dinner-time came the girl dressed herself, smoothed her yellow curls, and went shyly down the great staircase into the dining-room. It must be confessed that she glanced a little curiously at the table, wondering whether she was to dine alone or in company. This problem was soon solved; a side-door burst open, and Guy made his appearance, looking shy and ashamed of it as he came up and shook hands with her. "Miss Belinda," said he, "will you allow me to dine with you?"

"You must do as you like," said Belinda, quickly, starting back.

"Not at all," said Mr. Griffiths. "It is entirely as you shall decide. If you don't like my company, you need only say so. I shall not be offended. Well, shall we dine together?"

"Oh, certainly," laughed Belinda, confused in her turn.

So the two sat down to dine together. For the first time in his life Guy thought the great room light enough and bright and comfortable. The gold and silver plate didn't seem to crush him, nor the draperies to suffocate, nor the great columns ready to fall upon him. There was Belinda picking her grapes and playing with the sugar-plums. He could hardly believe it possible. His poor old heart gave great wistful thumps (if such a thing is possible) at the sound of her voice. She had lost much of her shyness, and they were talking of anything that came into their heads. She had been telling him about Myrtle Cottage, and the spiders there, and looking up, laughing, she was surprised to see him staring at her very sadly and kindly. He turned away abruptly, and began to help himself to all sorts of things out of the silver dishes.

"It's very good of you," Guy said, looking away, "to come and brighten this dismal house, and to stay with a poor suffering woman and a great uncouth fellow like myself."

"But you are both so very kind," said Belinda, simply. "I shall never forget — "

"Kind!" cried Guy, very roughly. "I behaved like a brute to you and your father yesterday. I am not used to ladies' society. I am stupid and shy and awkward."

"If you were very stupid," said Belle, smiling, "you would not have said that, Mr. Griffiths. Stupid people always think themselves charming."

When Guy said good-night immediately after dinner, as usual, he sighed again, and looked at her with such kind and melancholy eyes that Belle felt an odd affection and compassion for him. "I never should have thought it possible to like him so much," thought the girl, as she slowly went along the passage to Mrs. Griffiths' door.

It was an odd life this young creature led in the great silent, stifling house, with uncouth Guy for her playfellow, the sick woman's complaints and fancies for her duty in life. The silence of it all, its very comfort and splendidness, oppressed Belinda more at times than a simpler and more busy life. But the garden was an endless pleasure and refreshment, and she used to stroll about, skim over the terraces and walks, smell the roses, feed the birds and the goldfishes. Sometimes I have stood at my window, watching the active figure flitting by in and out under the trellis, fifteen times round the pond, thirty-two times along the terrace walk. Belle was obliged to set herself tasks, or she would have got tired sometimes of wandering about by herself. All this time she never thought of Guy except as a curious sort of companion; any thought of sentiment had never once occurred to her.

VI.

One day that Belle had been in the garden longer than usual, she remembered a note for Mrs. Griffiths that she had forgotten to write, and springing up the steps into the hall, on the way, with some roses in her apron, she suddenly almost ran up against Guy, who had come home earlier than usual.

The girl stood blushing and looking more charming than ever. The young fellow stood quite still, too, looking with such expressive and admiring glances that Belinda blushed deeper still, and made haste to escape to her room. Presently the gong sounded, and there was no help for it, and she had to go down again. Guy was in the dining-room as polite and as shy as usual, and Belinda gradually forgot the passing impression. The butler put the dessert on the table and left them, and when she had finished her fruit Belinda got up to say good-by. As she was leaving the room she heard Guy's footsteps following. She stopped short. He came up to her. He looked very pale, and said suddenly, in a quick, husky voice, —

"Belle, will you marry me?"

Poor Belinda opened her gray eyes full in his face. She could hardly believe she had heard aright. She was startled, taken aback, but she followed her impulse of the moment, and answered gravely, —

"No, Guy."

He wasn't angry or surprised. He had known it all along, poor fellow, and expected nothing else. He only sighed, looked at her once again, and then went away out of the room.

Poor Belle! she stood there where he had left her, — the lights burned, the great table glittered, the curtains waved. It was like a strange dream. She clasped her hands together, and then suddenly ran and fled away up to her own room,— frightened, utterly puzzled, bewildered, not knowing what to do or to whom to speak. It was a comfort to be summoned as usual to read to Mrs. Griffiths. She longed to pour out her story to the poor lady, but she dreaded agitating her. She read as she was bid. Once she stopped short, but her mistress impatiently motioned her to go on. She obeyed, stumbling and tumbling over the words before her, until there came a knock at the door, and, contrary to his custom, Guy entered the room. He looked very pale, poor fellow, and sad and subdued.

"I wanted to see you, Miss Belinda," he said aloud, " and to tell you that I hope this will make no difference, and that you will remain with us as if nothing had happened. You warned me, mamma, but I could not help myself. It's my own fault. Good-night. That is all I had to say."

Belle turned wistfully to Mrs. Griffiths. The thin hand was impatiently twisting the coverlet.

"Of course,—who would have anything to say to him? Foolish fellow!" she muttered, in her indistinct way. "Go on, Miss Barly."

"Oh, but tell me first, ought I to remain here?" Belle asked, imploringly.

"Certainly, unless you are unhappy with us," the sick woman answered, peevishly. Mrs. Griffiths never made any other allusion to what had happened. I think the truth was that she did not care very much for anything outside the doors of her sick-room. Perhaps she thought her son had been over-hasty, and that in time Belinda might change her mind. To people lying on their last sick-beds, the terrors, anxieties, longings of life seem very curious and strange. They seem to forget that they were once anxious, hopeful, eager themselves, as they lie gazing at the awful veil which will so soon be withdrawn from before their fading eyes.

A sort of constraint came between Guy and Belinda at first, but it wore away by degrees. He often alluded to his proposal, but in so hopeless and gentle a way that she could not be angry; still she was disquieted and unhappy. She felt that it was a false and awkward position. She could not bear to see him looking ill and sad, as he did at times, with great black rings under his dark eyes. It was worse still when she saw him brighten up with happiness at some chance word she let fall now and then,—speaking inadvertently of home, as he did, or of the roses next year. He must not mistake her. She could not bear to pain him by hard words, and yet sometimes she felt it was her duty to speak them. One day she met him in the street, on her way back to the house. The roll of the passing carriage-wheels gave Guy confidence, and, walking by her side, he began to say,—

"Now I never know what delightful surprise may not be waiting for me at every street corner. Ah, Miss Belle, my whole life might be one long dream of wonder and happiness, if . . ."

"Don't speak like this ever again; I shall go away," said Belle, interrupting, and crossing the road, in her agitation, under the very noses of two omnibus horses. "I wish I could like you enough to marry you. I shall always love you enough to be your friend; please don't talk of anything else."

Belle said this in a bright, brisk, imploring, decided way, and hoped to have put an end to the matter. That day she came to me and told her little story. There were almost as many reasons for her staying as for her leaving, the poor child thought. I could not advise her to go, for the assistance that she was able to send home was very valuable. Guy laughed, and utterly refused to accept a sixpence of her salary. Mrs. Griffiths evidently wanted her; Guy, poor fellow, would have given all he had to keep her, as we all knew too well.

Circumstance orders events sometimes, when people themselves, with all their powers and knowledge of good and of evil, are but passive instruments in the hands of fate. News came that Mr. Barly was ill, and little Belinda, with an anxious face, and a note in her trembling hand, came into Mrs. Griffiths' room one day to say she must go to him directly.

"Your father is ill," wrote Anna. "Circumstances demand your immediate return to him."

Guy happened to be present, and, when Belle left the room, he followed her out into the passage.

"You are going!" he said.

"I don't know what Anna means by circumstances, but papa is ill, and wants me," said Belinda, almost crying.

"And I want you," said Guy; "but that don't matter, of course. Go,—go, since you wish it."

After all, perhaps it was well she was going, thought Belle, as she went to pack up her boxes. Poor Guy's sad face haunted her. She seemed to carry it away in her box with her other possessions.

It would be difficult to describe what he felt, poor fellow, when he came upon the luggage standing ready corded in the hall, and he found that Belle had taken him at his word. He was so silent a man, so self-contained, so diffident of his own strength to win her love in time, so unused to the ways of the world and of women, that he could be judged by no ordinary rule. His utter despair and bewilderment would have been laughable almost, if they had not been so genuine. He paced about the garden with hasty, uncertain footsteps, muttering to himself as he went along, and angrily cutting at the rose-hedges. "Of course she must go, since she wished it; of course she must—of course, of course. What would the house be like when she was gone?" For an instant a vision of a great dull vault without warmth, or light, or color, or possible comfort anywhere, rose before him. He tried to imagine what his life would be if she never came back into it; but as he stood still, trying to seize the picture, it seemed to him that it was a thing not to be imagined or thought of. Wherever he looked he saw her, everywhere and in everything. He had imagined himself unhappy; now he discovered that for the last few weeks, since little Belinda had come, he had basked in the summer she had brought, and found new life in the sunshine of her presence. Of an evening he had come home eagerly from his daily toil looking to find her. When he left early in the morning, he would look up with kind eyes at her windows as he drove away. Once, early one morning, he had passed her near the lodge-gate, standing in the shadow of the great aspen-tree, and making way for the horses to go by. Belle was holding back the clean, stiff folds of her pink muslin dress; she looked up with that peculiar blink of her gray eyes, smiled and nodded her bright head, and shrunk away from the horses. Every morning Guy used to look under the tree after that to see if she were there by chance, even if he had parted from her but a minute before. Good, stupid old fellow! he used to smile to himself at his own foolishness. One of his fancies about her was that Belinda was a bird who would fly away some day, and perch up in the branches of one of the great trees, far, far beyond his reach. And now was this fancy coming true? was she going — leaving him — flying away where he could not follow her? He gave an inarticulate sound of mingled anger and sorrow and tenderness, which relieved his heart, but which puzzled Belle herself, who was coming down the garden-walk to meet him.

"I was looking for you, Mr. Griffiths," said Belle. "Your mother wants to speak to you. I, too, wanted to ask you something," the girl went on, blushing. "She is kind enough to wish me to come back. . . . But — "

Belle stopped short, blushed up, and began pulling at the leaves sprouting on either side of the narrow alley. When she looked up after a minute, with one of her quick, short-sighted glances, she found that Guy's two little brown eyes were fixed upon her steadily.

"Don't be afraid that I shall trouble you," he said, reddening. "If you knew — if you had the smallest conception what your presence is to me, you would come back. I think you would."

Miss Barly didn't answer, but blushed up again and walked on in silence, hanging her head to conceal the two bright tears which had come into her eyes. She was sorry, so very sorry. But what could she do? Guy had walked on to the end of the rose-garden, and Belle had followed. Now, instead of turning towards the house, he had come out into the bright-looking kitchen-garden, with its red brick walls hung with their various draperies of lichen and mosses, and garlands of clambering fruit. Four little paths led up to the turf-carpet which had been laid down in the centre of the garden. Here a fountain plashed with a tranquil fall of waters upon water; all sorts of sweet kitchen-herbs, mint and thyme and parsley, were growing along the straight-cut beds. Birds were pecking at the nets along the walls; one little sparrow that had been drinking at the fountain flew away as they approached. The few bright-colored straggling flowers caught the sunlight and reflected it in sparks like the water.

The master of this pleasant place put out his great, clumsy hand, and took hold of Belle's soft, reluctant fingers.

"Ah, Belle," he said, "is there no hope for me? Will there never be any chance?"

"I wish with all my heart there was a chance," said poor Belle, pulling away her hand impatiently. "Why do you wound and pain me by speaking again and again of what is far best forgotten? Dear Mr. Griffiths, I will marry you to-morrow, if you desire it," said the girl, with a sudden impulse, turning pale and remembering all that she owed to his forbearance and gentleness; "but please, please don't ask it." She looked so frightened and desperate that poor Guy felt that this was worse than anything, and sadly shook his head.

"Don't be afraid," he said. "I don't want to marry you against your will, or keep you here. Yes, you shall go home, and I will stop here alone, and cut my throat if I find I cannot bear the place without you. I am only joking. I dare say I shall do very well," said Griffiths, with a sigh; and he turned away and began stamping off in his clumsy way.

Then he suddenly stopped and looked back. Belle was standing in the sunshine with her face hidden in her hands. She was so puzzled, and sorry, and hopeless, and mournful. The only thing she could do was to cry, poor child, — and by some instinct Griffiths guessed that she was crying; he knew it, — his heart melted with pity. The poor fellow came back trembling. "My dearest," he said, "don't cry. What a brute I am to make you cry! Tell me anything in the whole world I can do to make you happy."

"If I could only do anything for you," said Belle, "that would make me happier."

"Then come back, my dear," said Guy, "and don't fly away yet forever, as you threatened just now. Come back and cheer up my mother, and make tea and a little sunshine for me, until — until some confounded fellow comes and carries you off," said poor Griffiths.

"Oh, that will never be. Yes, I'll come," said Belle, earnestly. "I'll go home for a week and come back; indeed I will."

"Only let me know," said Mr. Griffiths, "and my mother will send the carriage for you. Shall we say a week?" he added, anxious to drive a hard bargain.

"Yes," said Belinda, smiling; "I'll write and tell you the day."

Nothing would induce Griffiths to order the carriage until after dinner, and it was quite late at night when Belle got home.

———

VII.

POOR little Myrtle Cottage looked very small and shabby as she drove up in the darkness to the door. A brilliant illumination streamed from all the windows. Martha rubbed her elbows at the sight of the gorgeous equipage. Fanny came to the door surprised, laughing, giggling, mysterious. Everything looked much as usual, except that a large and pompous-looking gentleman was sitting on the drawing-room sofa, and beside him Anna, with a huge ring on her fourth finger, attempting to blush as Belle came into the room. Belle saw that she was not wanted, and ran upstairs to her father, who was better, and sitting in the arm-chair by his bedside. The poor old man nearly cried with delight and surprise, held out both his shaking hands to her, and clung tenderly to the bright young daughter. Belle sat beside him, holding his hand, asking him a hundred questions, kissing his wrinkled face and cheeks, and telling him all that had happened. Mr. Barly, too, had news to give. The fat gentleman downstairs, he told Belle, was no other than Anna's old admirer, the doctor, of whom mention has been made. He had re-proposed the day before, and was now sitting on the sofa on probation. Fanny's pros-

pects, too, seemed satisfactory. "She assures me," said Mr. Barly, "that young Ogden is on the point of coming forward. An old man like me, my dear, is naturally anxious to see his children settled in life and comfortably provided for. I don't know who would be good enough for my Belinda. Not that awkward lout of a Griffiths. No, no; we must look out better than that."

"O papa, if you knew how good and how kind he is!" said Belle, with a sudden revulsion of feeling; but she broke off abruptly, and spoke of something else.

The other maid, who had already gone to bed the night before when Belle arrived at the cottage, gave a loud shriek when she went into the room next morning and found some one asleep in the bed. Belle awoke, laughed and explained, and asked her to bring up her things.

"Bring 'em hup?" said the girl. "What, all them 'ampers that's come by the cart? No, miss, that's more than me and Martha have the strength for. I should crick my back if I were to attempt for to do such a thing."

"Hampers,—what hampers?" Belle asked; but when she went down she found the little passage piled with cases, flowers, and game and preserves, and some fine old port for Mr. Barly, and some roses for Belle. As Belinda came downstairs, in her fresh morning dress, Anna, who had been poking about and examining the various packages, looked up with offended dignity.

"I think, considering that I am mistress here," said she, "these hampers should have been directed to me, instead of to you, Belinda. Mr. Griffiths strangely forgets. Indeed, I fear that you too are wanting in any great sense of ladylike propriety."

"Prunes, prism, propriety," said Belle, gayly. "Never mind, dear Anna; he's sent the things for all of us. Mr. Griffiths certainly never meant me to drink two dozen bottles of port wine in a week."

"You are evading the question," said Anna, "I have been wishing to talk to you for some time past, — come into the dining-room, if you please."

It seems almost impossible to believe, and yet I cannot help fearing that out of sheer spite and envy Anna Barly had even then determined that if she could prevent it, Belinda should never go back to Castle Gardens again, but remain in the cottage. The sight of the pretty things which had been given her there, all the evidences which told of the esteem and love in which she was held, maddened the foolish woman. I can give no other reason for the way in which she opposed Belinda's return to Mrs. Griffiths. "Her duty is at home," said Anna. "I myself shall be greatly engaged with Thomas," — so she had already learnt to call Dr. Robinson. "Fanny also is preoccupied; Belinda must remain."

When Belle demurred and said that for the next few weeks she would like to return as she had promised, and stay until Mrs. Griffiths was suited with another companion, Anna's indignation rose and overpowered her dignity. Was it her sister who was so oblivious of the laws of society, propriety, modesty? Anna feared that Belinda had not reflected upon the strange appearance her conduct must have to others, to the Ogdens, to them all. What was the secret attraction which took her back? Anna said she had rather not inquire, and went on with her oration. "Unmaidenly, — not to be thought of, — the advice of those whose experience might be trusted" — does one not know the rigmarole by heart? When even the father, who had been previously talked to, sided with his eldest daughter, when Thomas, who was also called into the family conclave, nodded his head in an ominous manner, poor little Belinda, frightened, shaken, undecided, almost promised that she would do as they desired; and as she promised, the thought of poor Guy's grief and wistful, haggard face came before her, and her poor little heart ached and sank at the thought. But not even Belinda, with all her courage, could resist the decision of so much experience, or Anna's hints and innuendoes, or, more insurmountable than all the rest, a sudden shyness and consciousness which had come over the poor little maiden, who turned crimson with shame and annoyance.

Belinda had decided as she was told, — had done as her conscience bid her, — and yet there was but little satisfaction in this duty accomplished. For about half an hour she went about feeling like a heroine, and then without any reason or occasion, it seemed to her that the mask had come off her face, that she had discovered herself to be a traitoress, that she had betrayed and abandoned her kindest friends; she called herself a selfish, ungrateful wretch, she wondered what Guy would think of her; she was out of temper, out of spirits, out of patience with herself, and the click of the blind swinging in the draft was unendurable. The complacent expression of

Anna's handsome face put her teeth on edge. When Fanny tumbled over the footstool with a playful shriek, to everybody's surprise Belinda burst out crying.

Those few days were endless, slow, dull, unbearable,— every second brought its pang of regret and discomfort and remorse. It seemed to Belinda that her ears listened, her mouth talked, her eyes looked at the four walls of the cottage, at the furze on the common, at the faces of her sisters, with a sort of mechanical effort. As if she were acting her daily life, not living it naturally and without effort. Only when she was with her father did she feel unconstrained; but even then there was an unexpressed reproach in her heart like a dull pain that she could not quiet. And so the long days lagged. Although Dr. Robinson enlivened them with his presence, and the Ogdens drove up to carry Fanny off to the happy regions of Capulet Square (E. for Elysium Anna I think would have docketed the district), to Belinda those days seemed slow, and dark, and dim, and almost hopeless at times.

On the day on which Belinda was to have returned, there came a letter to me telling her story plainly enough. "I must not come back, my dearest Miss Williamson," she wrote. "I am going to write to Mrs. Griffiths and dear, kind Mr. Guy to-morrow to tell them so. Anna does not think it is right. Papa clings to me and wants me, now that both my sisters are going to leave him. How often I shall think of you all, — of all your goodness to me, of the beautiful roses, and my dear little room! Do you think Mr. Guy would let me take one or two books as a remembrance — Hume's History of England, Porteous's Sermons, and Essays on Reform? I should like to have something to remind me of you all, and to see sometimes, since they say I am not to see you all again. Good-by, and thank you and Mrs. H. a thousand, thousand times. Your ever, ever affectionate BELINDA. P. S. Might I also ask for that little green volume of the Golden Treasury which is up in the tower-room?"

This was what Guy had feared all along. Once she was gone, he knew by instinct she would never come back. I hardly know how it fared with the poor fellow all this time. He kept out of our way, and would try to escape me; but once by chance I met him, and I was shocked by the change which had come over him. I had my own opinion, as we all have at times. H. and I had talked it over, — for old women are good for something, after all, and can sometimes play a sentimental part in life as well as young ones. It seemed to us impossible that Belinda should not relent to so much goodness and unselfishness, and come back again some day, never to go any more. We knew enough of Anna Barly to guess the part *she* had played, nor did we despair of seeing Belinda among us once more. But some one must help her; she could not reach us unassisted; and so I told Mrs. Griffiths, who had remarked upon her son's distress and altered looks.

"If you will lend us the carriage," I said, "either H. or I will go over to Dumbleton to-morrow, and I doubt not that we shall bring her."

H. went. She told me about it afterwards. Anna was fortunately absent. Mr. Barly was downstairs, and H. was able to talk to him a little bit before Belinda came down. The poor old man always thought as he was told to think, and since his illness he was more uncertain and broken than ever. He was dismayed when H. told him in her decided way that he was probably sacrificing two people's happiness for life by his ill-timed interference. When at last Belinda came down, she looked almost as ill as Griffiths himself. She rushed into H.'s arms with a scream of delight, and eagerly asked a hundred questions. "How were they all — what were they all doing?"

H. was very decided. Everybody was very ill and wanted Belinda back. "Your father says he can spare you very well," said she. "Why not come back with me this afternoon, if only for a time? It is your duty," H. continued, in her dry way. "You should not leave them in this uncertainty."

"Go, my child; pray go," urged Mr. Barly.

And at last Belinda consented shyly, nothing loth.

H. began to question her when she had got her safe in the carriage. Belinda said she had not been well. She could not sleep, she said. She had had bad dreams. She blushed and confessed that she had dreamed of Guy lying dead in the kitchen-garden. She had gone about the house trying — indeed she had tried — to be cheerful and busy as usual, but she felt unhappy, ungrateful. "Oh, what a foolish girl I am!" she said.

All the lights were burning in the little town, the west was glowing and reflected in the river; the boats trembled and shot through the shiny waters, and the people were out upon the banks, as they crossed the bridge again on their way from Dumbleton. Belle was happier, certainly, but crying from agitation.

"Have I made him miserable, poor fellow? Oh, I think I shall blame myself all my life," said she, covering her face with her hands. "O H.! H.! what shall I do?"

H. dryly replied that she must be guided by circumstances, and, when they reached Castle Gardens, kissed her and set her down at the great gate, while she herself went home in the carriage.

It was all twilight by this time among the roses. Belinda met the gate-keeper, who touched his hat and told her his master was in the garden; and so, instead of going into the house, she flitted away towards the garden, crossed the lawns, and went in and out among the bowers and trellises looking for him, — frightened by her own temerity at first, gaining courage by degrees. It was so still, so sweet, so dark; the stars were coming out in the evening sky, a meteor went flashing from east to west, a bat flew across her path; all the scent hung heavy in the air. Twice Belinda called out timidly, "Mr. Griffiths, Mr. Griffiths!" but no one answered. Then she remembered her dream in sudden terror, and hurried into the kitchen-garden to the fountain where they had parted.

What had happened? Some one was lying on the grass. Was this her dream? was it Guy? was he dead? had she killed him? Belinda ran up to him, seized his hand, and called him Guy — dear Guy; and Guy, who had fallen asleep from very weariness and sadness of heart, opened his eyes to hear himself called by the voice he loved best in the world; while the sweetest eyes, full of tender tears, were gazing anxiously into his ugly face. Ugly? Fairy tales have told us this at least, that ugliness and dulness do not exist for those who truly love. Had she ever thought him rough, uncouth, unlovable? Ah! she had been blind in those days; she knew better now. As they walked back through the twilight garden that night, Guy said humbly, —

"I shan't do you any credit, Belinda; I can only love you."

"*Only!*"

She didn't finish her sentence; but he understood very well what she meant.

CINDERELLA.

BY

MISS THACKERAY,

AUTHOR OF "BEAUTY AND THE BEAST," "LITTLE RED RIDING HOOD," "JACK THE GIANT-KILLER," "THE SLEEPING BEAUTY IN THE WOOD," ETC.

LORING, Publisher,

319 WASHINGTON STREET,

BOSTON.

1867.

CINDERELLA.

It is, happily, not only in fairy tales that things sometimes fall out as one could wish, that anxieties are allayed, mistakes explained away, friends reconciled; that people inherit large fortunes, or are found out in their nefarious schemes; that long-lost children are discovered disguised in soot; that vessels come safely sailing into port after the storm; and that young folks who have been faithful to one another are married off at last. Some of these young couples are not only happily married, but they also begin life in pleasant palaces tastefully decorated, and with all the latest improvements; with convenient cupboards, bath-rooms, back-staircases, speaking-tubes, lifts from one story to another, hot and cold water laid on; while outside lie well-kept parks, and gardens, and flower-beds; and from the muslin-veiled windows they can see the sheep browsing, the long, shadowy grass, deer starting across the sunny glades, swans floating on the rivers, and sailing through the lilies and tall lithe reeds. There are fruit-gardens, too, where great purple plums are sunning on the walls, and cucumbers lying asleep among their cool, dark leaves. There are glass-houses where heavy, dropping bunches of grapes are hanging, so that one need only open one's mouth for them to fall into it all ready cooked and sweetened. Sometimes, in addition to all these good things, the young couple possess all the gracious gifts of youth, beauty, gay and amiable dispositions. Some one said, the other day, that it seemed as if Fate scarcely knew what she was doing, when she lavished with such profusion every gift and delight upon one pair of heads, while others were left bald, shorn, unheeded, dishevelled, forgotten, dishonored. And yet the world would be almost too sad to bear, if one did not sometimes see happiness somewhere. One would scarcely believe in its possible existence, if there was nobody young, fortunate, prosperous, delighted; nobody to think of

with satisfaction, and to envy a little. The sight of great happiness and prosperity is like listening to harmonious music, or looking at beautiful pictures, at certain times of one's life. It seems to suggest possibilities, it sets sad folks longing; but while they are wishing, still, may be, a little reproachfully, they realize the existence of what perhaps they had doubted before. Fate has been hard to them, but there is compensation even in this life. They tell themselves, "Which of us knows when his turn may come?" Happiness is a fact: it does lie within some people's grasp. To this or that young fairy couple, age, trial, and trouble may be in store; but now at least the present is golden; the innocent delights and triumphs of youth and nature are theirs.

I could not help moralizing a little in this way, when we were staying with young Lulworth and his wife the other day, coming direct from the struggling, dull atmosphere of home to the golden placidity of Lulworth farm. They drove us over to Cliffe Court, — another oasis, so it seemed to me, in the arid plains of life. Cliffe Court is a charming, cheerful, Italian-looking house, standing on a hill in the midst of a fiery furnace of geraniums and flower-beds. "It belongs to young Sir Charles Richardson. He is six-and-twenty, and the handsomest man in the county," said Frank.

"Oh, no, Frank; you are joking, surely," said Cecilia; and then she stared, and then blushed in her odd way. She still stared sometimes when she was shy, as she used to do before she married.

So much of her former habits Cecilia had also retained, that as the clock struck eight o'clock every morning a great, punctual breakfast-bell used to ring in the outer hall. The dining-room casement was wide open upon the beds of roses, the tea was made, Cecilia in her crisp white morning dress, and with all her wavy bronze hair curling about her face, was waiting to pour it out, the eggs were boiled, the bacon was frizzling hot upon the plate to a moment; there was no law allowed, not a minute's grace for anybody, no matter how lazy. They had been married a little more than two years, and were quite established in their country home. I wish I could perform some incantation like those of my friends, the fairies, and conjure up the old farm bodily with a magic wave of my pen, or by drawing a triangle with a circle through it upon the paper — as the enchanters do. The most remarkable things about the farm were its curious and beautiful old chimneys, — indeed the whole county of Sussex is celebrated for them, and the meanest little cottages have noble-looking stacks all ornamented, carved, and weather-beaten. There were gables also, and stony mullioned windows, and ancient steps with rusty rings hanging to them, affixed there to fasten the bridles of horses that would have run away several hundred years ago, if this precaution had not been taken. And then there were storehouses and ricks and barns, all piled with the abundance of the harvest. The farm-yard was alive with young fowls, and cocks and hens, and guinea-hens; those gentle little dowagers went about glistening in silver and gray, and Cecilia's geese came clamoring to meet her. I can see it all as I think about it. The old walls are all carved and ornamented, sometimes by art and work of man's hand, sometimes by time and lovely little natural mosses. House-leeks grow in clumps upon the thatch, a pretty girl is peeping through a lattice window, a door is open while a rush of sweet morning scent comes through the shining oaken passage from the herb-garden and orchard behind. Cows with their soft brown eyes and cautious tread are passing on their way to a field across the road. A white horse waiting by his stable door shakes his head and whinnies.

Frank and Cecilia took us for a walk after breakfast the first morning we came. We were taken to the stables first and the cow-houses, and then we passed out through a gate into a field, and crossing the field we got into a copse which skirted it, and so by many a lovely little winding path into the woods. Young Lulworth took our delight and admiration as a personal compliment. It was all Lulworth property as far as we could see. I thought it must be strangely delightful to be the possessor of such beautiful hills, mist, sunshine, and shadow, violet tones, song of birds, and shimmer of

foliage; but Frank, I believe, looked at his future prospects from a material point of view. "You see it aint the poetic part of it which pays," he said. But he appreciated it nevertheless, for Cecilia came out of the woods that morning, all decked out with great convolvulus leaves, changed to gold, which Frank had gathered as we went along and given to her. This year all the leaves were turning to such beautiful colors that people remarked upon it, and said they never remembered such a glowing autumn; even the year when Frank came to Dorlicote was not to compare to it. Browns and russet, and bright amber and gold flecks, berries, red leaves, a lovely blaze and glitter in the woods along the lanes and beyond the fields and copses. All the hills were melting with lovely color in the clear, warm autumn air, and the little nut-wood paths seemed like Aladdin's wonderful gardens, where precious stones hung to the trees. There was a twinkle and crisp shimmer, yellow leaves and golden light, yellow light and golden leaves, red hawthorn, convolvulus-berries, holly-berries beginning to glow, and heaped-up clustering purple blackberries. The sloe-berries, or snowy blackthorn fruit, with their soft gloom of color, were over, and this was the last feast of the year. On the trees the apples hung red and bright, the pears seemed ready to drop from their branches and walls, the wheat was stacked, the sky looked violet behind the yellow ricks. A blackbird was singing like a ripple of water, somebody said. It is hard to refrain from writing of all of these lovely things, though it almost is an impertinence to attempt to set them down on paper in long lists, like one of Messrs. Rippon and Burton's circulars. It seemed sad to be sad on such a morning and in such a world, but as we were walking along the high-road on our way back to the farm, we passed a long, pale, melancholy-looking man riding a big horse, with a little sweet-faced creature about sixteen who was cantering beside him. He took off his hat, the little girl kissed her hand as they passed, nodding a gay, triumphant nod, and then we watched them down the hill, and disappearing at the end of the lane.

"I am quite glad to see Ella Ashford out riding with her father again," said Lulworth, holding the garden-gate open for us to pass in.

"Mrs. Ashford called here a day or two ago with her daughter," said Cecilia. "They're going to stay at the Ravenhill, she told me. I thought Colonel Ashford, was gone, too. I suppose he is come back." "Of course he is," said Frank, "since we have just seen him with Ella, and of course his wife is away for the same reason."

"The child has grown very thin," said H.

"She has a difficult temper," said Cecilia, — who, once she got an idea into her soft, silly head, did not easily get rid of it again. "She is a great anxiety to poor Mrs. Ashford. She is very different, she tells me, to Julia and Lisette Garnier, her own daughters."

"I knew them when they were children. We used to see a great deal of Mrs. Ashford when she was first a widow, and I went to her second wedding."

We were at Paris one year, — ten years before the time I am writing of, — and Mrs. Garnier lived over us, in a tiny little apartment. She was very poor, and very grandly dressed, and she used to come rustling in to see us. Rustling is hardly the word, — she was much too graceful and womanly a person to rustle; her long silk gowns used to ripple and wave and flow away as she came and went; and her beautiful eyes used to fill with tears as she drank her tea and confided her troubles to us. H. never liked her; but I must confess to a very kindly feeling for the poor, gentle, beautiful, forlorn young creature, so passionately lamenting the loss she had sustained in Major-General Garnier. He had left her very badly off, although she was well connected, and Lady Jane Peppercorne, her cousin, had offered her and her two little girls a home at Ravenhill, she used to tell us in her eploré manner. I do not know why she never availed herself of the offer. She said once that she would not be doing justice to her precious little ones, to whom she devoted herself with the assistance of an experienced attendant. My impression is, that the little ones used to scrub one another's little ugly faces, and plait one another's little light Chinese-looking tails, while the experienced attendant laced and dressed and adorned, and scented and powdered their mamma. She really was a beautiful young woman, and would have looked quite charming if she had left herself alone for a single instant, but she was always posing. She had dark, bright eyes; she had a lovely little arched mouth; and hands so white, so soft, so covered with rings, that one felt that it was indeed a privilege when she said, "Oh, *how* do you do?" and extended

two or three gentle, confiding fingers. At first she went nowhere except to church, and to walk in the retired paths of the Park de Mongeau, although she took in *Galignani* and used to read the lists of arrivals. But by degrees she began to — chiefly to please me, she said — go out a little, to make a few acquaintances. One day I was walking with her down the Champs Elysées, when she suddenly started and looked up at a tall, melancholy-looking gentleman who was passing, and who stared at her very hard; and soon after that it was that she began telling me she had determined to make an effort for her children's sake, and to go a little more into society. She wanted me to take her to Madame de Girouette's, where she heard I was going that evening, and where she believed she should meet an old friend of hers, whom she particularly wished to see again. Would I help her? Would I be so *very* good? Of course I was ready to do anything I could. She came punctual to her time, all gray moire and black lace; a remise was sent for, and we set off, jogging along the crowded streets, with our two lamps lighted, and a surly man, in a red waistcoat and an oilskin hat, to drive us to the Rue de Lille. All the way there, Mrs. Garnier was strange, silent, nervous, excited. Her eyes were like two shining craters, I thought, when we arrived, and as we climbed up the interminable flights of stairs. I guessed who was the old friend with the gray mustache in a minute; a good, well-looking, sick-looking man, standing by himself in a corner.

I spent a curious evening, distracted between Madame de Girouette's small talk, to which I was supposed to be listening, and Mrs. Garnier's murmured conversation with her old friend in the corner, to which I was vainly endeavoring not to attend.

"My dear, imagine a *bouillon*, surmounted with little tiny flutings all round the bottom, and then three *ruches*, alternating with three little *volants*, with great *choux* at regular intervals; over this a tunic, caught up at the side by a *jardinière*, a *ceinture à la Bébé.*"

"When you left us I was a child, weak, foolish, easily frightened and influenced. It nearly broke my heart. Look me in the face, if you can, and tell me you do not believe me," I heard Mrs. Garnier murmuring in a low, thrilling whisper. She did not mean me to hear it, but she was too absorbed in what she was saying to think of all the people round about her.

"Ah, Lydia, what does it matter now?" the friend answered in a sad voice, which touched me somehow. "We have both been wrecked in our ventures, and life has not much left for either of us now."

"It is cut en biais," Madame de Girouette went on; "the pieces which are taken out at one end are let in at the other; the effect is quite charming, and the economy is immense."

"For you, you married the person you loved," Lydia Garnier was answering; "for me, out of the wreck, I have at least my children, and a remembrance, and a friend, —is it so? Ah, Henry, have I not at least a friend?"

"Everybody wants one," said Madame de Girouette, concluding her conversation, "and they cannot be made fast enough to supply the demand. I am promised mine to wear to-morrow at the opening of the salon, but I am afraid that you have no chance. How the poor thing is overworked! —her magazin is crowded—I believe she will leave it all in charge of her première demoiselle, and retire to her campagne as soon as the season is over."

"And you will come and see me, will you not?" said the widow, as we went away, looking up. I do not know to this day if she was acting. I believe, to do her justice, that she was only acting what she really felt, as many of us do at times.

I took Mrs. Garnier home as I had agreed. I did not ask any questions. I met Colonel Ashford on the stairs next day, and I was not surprised when, about a week after, Mrs. Garnier came into the drawing-room early one morning, sinking down at my feet in a careless attitude, seized my hand, and said that she had come for counsel, for advice. She had had an offer from a person whom she respected, Colonel Ashford, whom I might have remarked that night at Madame de Girouette's; would I—would I give her my candid opinion; for her children's sake did I not think it would be well to think seriously? . . . .

"And for your own, too, my dear," said I. "Colonel Ashford is in Parliament; he is very well off. I believe you will be making an excellent marriage. Accept him, by all means."

"Dear friend, since this is your real, heartfelt opinion, I value your judgment too highly not to act by its dictates. Once, years ago, there was thought of this between me and Henry. I will now confide to you, my heart has never failed from its

early devotion. A cruel fate separated us. I married. He married. We are brought together as by a miracle, but our three children will never know the loss of their parents' love," etc. etc. Glance, hand-pressure, etc.—tears, etc. Then a long, soft, irritating kiss. I felt for the first time in my life inclined to box her ears.

The little Garniers certainly gained by the bargain, and the colonel sat down to write home to his little daughter, and tell her the news.

Poor little Ella,—I wonder what sort of anxieties Mrs. Ashford had caused to her before she had been Ella's father's wife a year. Miss Ashford made the best of it. She was a cheery, happy little creature, looking at everything from the sunny side, adoring her father, running wild out of doors, but with an odd turn for house-keeping, and order and method at home. Indeed, for the last two years, ever since she was twelve years old, she had kept her father's house. Languid, gentle, easily impressed, Colonel Ashford was quite curiously influenced by this little daughter. She could make him come and go, and like and dislike. I think it was Ella who sent him into Parliament; she could not bear Sir Rainham Richardson, their next neighbor, to be an M. P., and an oracle, while her father was only a retired colonel. Her ways and her sayings were a strange and pretty mixture of childishness and precociousness. She would be ordering dinner, seeing that the fires were alight in the study and dining-room, writing notes to save her father trouble (Colonel Ashford hated trouble), in her cramped, crooked, girlish hand; the next minute she was, perhaps, flying, agile-footed, round and round the old hall, skipping up and down the oak stairs, laughing out like a child as she played with her puppy, and dangled a little ball of string under his black nose. Puff, with a youthful bark, would seize the ball and go scuttling down the corridors with his prize, while Ella pursued him with her quick flying feet. She could sing charmingly, with a clear, true, piping voice, like a bird's, and she used to dance to her own singing in the prettiest way imaginable. Her dancing was really remarkable; she had the most beautiful feet and hands, and as she seesawed in time, still singing and moving in rhythm, any one seeing her could not fail to have been struck by the weird-like little accomplishment. Some girls have a passion for dancing; boys have a hundred other ways and means of giving vent to their activity and exercising their youthful limbs, and putting out their eager young strength; but girls have no such chances; they are condemned to walk through life for the most part quietly, soberly, putting a curb on the life and vitality which is in them. They long to throw it out, they would like to have wings to fly like a bird, and so they dance sometimes with all their hearts and might and energy. People rarely talk of the poetry of dancing, but there is something in it of the real inspiration of art. The music plays, the heart beats time, the movements flow as naturally as the branches of a tree go waving in the wind. . . .

One day a naughty boy, who had run away, for a lark, from his tutor and his school-room at Cliffe, hard by, and who was hiding in a ditch, happened to see Ella alone in a field. She was looking up at the sky, and down at the pretty scarlet and white pimpernels, and listening to the birds. Suddenly she felt so strong and so light, and as if she *must* jump about a little, she was so happy; and so she did, shaking her pretty golden mane, waving her poppies high over head, and singing higher and higher, like one of the larks that were floating in mid air. The naughty boy was much frightened, and firmly believed that he had seen a fairy. "She was all in white," he said afterwards, in an aggrieved tone of voice. "She'd no hat, or anything, — she bounded six foot into the air. You never saw anything like it."

Master Richardson's guilty conscience had something to do with his alarm. When his friend made a few facetious inquiries he answered quite sulkily, "Black pudden? she offered me no pudden or anything else. I only wish you had been there, that's all, then you'd believe a fellow when he says a thing, instead of always chaffing."

Ella gave up her dancing after the new wife came to Ash Place. It was all so different. She was not allowed any more to run out in the fields alone. She supposed it was very nice having two young companions like Lisette and Julia; and, at first, in her kindly way, the child did the honors of her own home, showed them the way which led to her rabbits, her most secret bird's nest, the old ivy-grown smugglers' hole in the hollow. Lisette and Julia went trotting about in their frill trousers and Chinese tails of hair, examining everything, making their calculations, saying nothing, taking it all in.

Poor little Ella was rather puzzled, and could not make them out. Meantime her new mother was gracefully wandering over the house on her husband's arm, and standing in attitudes, admiring the view from the windows, and asking gentle little indifferent questions, to all of which Colonel Ashford replied, unsuspectingly enough.

"And so you give the child an allowance. Is she not very young for one? And is this Ella's room? How prettily it is furnished!"

"She did it all herself," said her father, smiling. "Look at her rocking-horse, and her dolls' house, and her tidy little arrangements."

The house-keeping books were in a little pile on the table; a very suspicious-looking doll was lying on the bed, so were a pile of towels, half marked, but neatly foided; there was a bird singing in a cage, a squirrel, a little aged dog — Puff's grandmother — asleep on a cushion, some sea-anemones in a glass, gaping with their horrid mouths; strings of birds' eggs were suspended, and whips were hanging up on the walls. There was a great bunch of flowers in the window, and a long daisy-chain fastened up in festoons round the glass; and then on the toilet-table there were one or two valuable trinkets set out in their little cases.

"Dear me!" said Mrs. Ashford, "is it not a pity to leave such temptation in the way of the servants? Little careless thing!— had I not better keep them for her, Henry? They are very beautiful." And Mrs. Ashford softly collected Ella's treasures in her long white hands.

"Ella has some very valuable things," Colonel Ashford said. "She keeps them locked up in a strong box, I believe; yes, there it is in the corner."

"It had much better come into my closet," Mrs. Ashford said. "Oh, how heavy! Come here, strong-arm, and help me." Colonel Ashford obediently took up the box as he was bid.

"And I think I may as well finish marking the dusters," said Mrs. Ashford, looking round the room as she collected them all in her apron. "The books, of course, are now my duty. I think Ella will not be sorry to be relieved of her cares. Do you know, dear, I think I am glad, for her sake, that you married me, as well as for my own. I think she has had too much put upon her, is a little too decided, too *prononcée* for one so young. One would not wish to see her grow up before the time. Let them remain young and careless while they can, Henry."

So when Ella came back to mark the dusters that she had been hemming, because Mrs. Milton was in a hurry for them, and the housemaid had hurt her eye, they were gone, and so were her neat little books that she had taken such pride in, and had been winding up to give to Mrs. Ashford to keep in future; so was her pretty coral necklace that she wore of an evening, and her pearls with the diamond clasp, and her beautiful clear carbuncle brooch that she was so fond of, and her little gold-clasp bracelet. Although Eliza and Susan had lived with them all her life long, *they* had never taken her things, poor Ella thought, a little bitterly. "Quite unsuitable at your age, dearest," Mrs. Ashford murmured, kissing her fondly.

And Ella never got them back any more. Many and many other things there were she never got back, poor child. Ah me! treasures dearer to her than the pretty coral necklace and the gold-clasp bracelet, — liberty, confidence, the tender atmosphere of admiring love in which she had always lived, the first place in her father's heart. That should never be hers again some one had determined.

The only excuse for Mrs. Ashford is that she was very much in love with her husband, and so selfishly attached to him that she grudged the very care and devotion which little Ella had spent upon her father all these years past. Every fresh proof of thought and depth of feeling in such a childish little creature hurt and vexed the other woman. Ella must be taught her place, this lady determined, not in so many words. Alas! if we could always set our evil thoughts and schemes to work, it would perhaps be well with us, and better far than drifting, unconscious and unwarned, into nameless evil, unowned to one's self, scarcely recognized.

And so the years went by. Julia and Lisette grew up into two great, tall, fashionable, bouncing young ladies. They pierced their ears, turned up their pigtails, and dressed very elegantly. Lisette used to wear a coral necklace; Julia was partial to a clear carbuncle brooch her mother gave her. Little Ella, too, grew up like a little green plant springing up through the mild spring rains and the summer sunshine, taller and prettier and sadder every year. And yet perhaps it was as well, after all, that early in life she had to learn to be content with a very little share of its bounties. She might have been spoiled and over-in-

dulged if things had gone on as they began, if nothing had ever thwarted her, and if all her life she had had her own way. She was a bright, smiling little thing, for all her worries, with a sweet little face. Indeed, her beauty was so remarkable, and her manner so simple and charming, that Julia and Lisette, who were a year or two her elders, used to complain to their mother that nobody ever noticed them when Ella was by. Lady Jane Peppercorne, their own cousin, was always noticing her, and actually gave her a potato off her own plate the other day.

"I fear she is a very forward, designing girl. I shall not think of taking her out in London, this year," Mrs. Ashford said with some asperity; "nor shall I allow her to appear at our cróquet party next week. She is far too young to be brought out."

So Ella was desired to remain in her own room on this occasion. She nearly cried, poor little thing, but what could she do? Her father was away; and when he came back, Mrs. Ashford would be sure to explain everything to him. Mrs. Ashford had explained life in so strangely ingenious a manner that he had got to see it in a very topsy-turvy fashion. Some things she had explained away altogether, some she had distorted and twisted; poor little Ella had been explained and explained, until there was scarcely anything of her left at all. Poor child! she sometimes used to think she had not a single friend in the world; but she would chide herself for such fancies, — it must be fancy. Her father loved her as much as ever; but he was engrossed by business, and it was not to be expected he should show what he felt before Julia and Lisette, who might be hurt. And then Ella would put all her drawers in order, or sew a seam, or go out and pull up a bedful of weeds, to chase such morbid fancies out of her mind.

Lady Jane Peppercorne, of whom mention has already been made, had two houses, one in Onslow Square, another at Hampstead. She was very rich; she had never married, and was consequently far more sentimental than ladies of her standing usually are. She was a flighty old lady, and lived sometimes at one house, sometimes at the other, sometimes at hotels here and there, as the fancy seized her. She was very kind as well as flighty, and was constantly doing generous things, and trying to help any one who seemed to be in trouble, or who appeared to wish for anything she had it in her power to grant.

So when Mrs. Ashford said, "O Lady Jane, pity me! My husband says he cannot afford to take me to town this year. I should so like to go, for the dear girls' sake, of course, —" Lady Jane gave a little grunt, and said, "I will lend you my house in Onslow Square, if you like, — that is, if you keep my room ready for me in case I want to come up at any time. But I dare say you won't care for such an unfashionable quarter of the world."

"O Lady Jane, how exceedingly kind! how very delightful and unexpected!" cried Mrs. Ashford, who had been hoping for it all the time, and who hastened to communicate the news to Lisette and Julia.

"I shall want a regular outfit, mamma," said Julia, who was fond of dress. "Perhaps we shall meet young Mr. Richardson in town."

"I shall be snapped up directly by some one, I expect," said Lisette, who was very vain, and thought herself irresistible.

"Am I to come, too?" asked Ella, timidly, from the other end of the room, looking up from her sewing.

"I do not know," replied her stepmother, curtly, and Ella sighed a little wistfully, and went on stitching.

"At what age shall you let me come out?" she presently asked, shyly.

"When you are fit to be trusted in the world, and have cured your unruly temper," said Mrs. Ashford. Ella's eyes filled with tears, and she blushed up; but her father came into the room, and she smiled through her tears, and thought to herself that since her temper was so bad, she had better begin to rule it that very instant. . . . .

It is a bright May morning after a night of rain; and, although this is London and not the country any more, Onslow Square looks bright and clean. Lady Jane has had the house smartly done up; clean chintz, striped blinds, a balcony full of mignonette. She has kept two little rooms for herself and her maid; but all the rest of the house is at the Ashfords' disposal. Everybody is satisfied, and Ella is enchanted with her little room upstairs. Mrs. Ashford is making lists of visits and dinner-parties and milliner's addresses. Lisette is looking out of the window at some carriages which are passing; the children and nurses are sitting under the trees in the square; Julia is looking at herself in the glass, and practising

her court curtseys; and Ella is in the back-room, arranging a great heap of books in a book-case. "I should so like to go to the palace, mamma," she says, and looking up with a smudgy face, for the books were all dirty and covered with dust. "Do you think there will be room for me?"

Ella had no proper pride, as it is called, and always used to take it for granted she was wanted, and that some accident prevented her from going with the others. "I am sorry there is no room for you, Ella," said Mrs. Ashford, in her deep voice. "I have asked Mr. Richardson to come with us, and if he fails, I promised to call for the Countess Bricabrac. Pray, if you do not care for walking in the square this afternoon, see that my maid puts my things properly away in the cupboards, as well as Julia's and Lisette's, and help her to fold the dresses, because it is impossible for one person to manage these long trains unassisted."

"Very well," said Ella, cheerfully. "I hope you will have a pleasant day. How nice it must be to be going!"

"I wish you would learn not to wish for everything and anything that you happen to hear about, Ella," said Mrs. Ashford. "If you hear any visitors coming, go away, for I cannot allow you to be seen in this dirty state."

"There's a ring," said Ella, gathering some of the books together. "Good-by."

Young Mr. Richardson, who was announced immediately after, passed a pretty maid-servant, carrying a great pile of folios, upon the stairs. She looked so little fitted for the task that he involuntarily stopped and said, "Can I assist you?" The little maid smiled, and shook her head, without speaking. "What a charming little creature!" thought Mr. Richardson. He came to say that he and his friend, Jack Prettyman, were going to ride down together, and would join the ladies at the Palace.

"We are to pick Colonel Ashford up at his club," Mrs. Ashford said, "and Madame de Bricabrac. I shall count upon you then." And the young ladies waved him gracious au revoirs from the balcony.

"Oh! don't you like white waistcoats, Julia?" said Lisette, as she watched him down the street. •

They are gone. Ella went up to help with the dresses, but presently the maid said in her rude way that she must go down to dinner, and she could not have anybody messing the things about while she was away. Carter hated having a "spy" set over her, as she called Miss Ashford. The poor little spy went back to the drawing-room. She was too melancholy and out of spirits to dress herself and go out. Her face was still smudgy, and she had cried a little over Lisette's pink tarlatane. Her heart sank down, down, down. She did so long for a little fun and delight, and laughter and happiness. She knew her father would say, "Where is Ella?" and her mother would answer, "I really cannot account for Ella's fancies! Oh, she was sulky this morning again. I cannot manage her strange tempers."

The poor child chanced to see her shabby face and frock and tear-stained cheeks in one of the tall glasses over the gilt tables. It was very silly, but the woebegone little face touched her so; she was so sorry for it that all of a sudden she burst out sob, sob, sob, crying. "Oh, how nice it must be to be loved and cherished, and very happy!" she thought. "Oh, I could be so good if they would only love me!" She could not bear to think more directly of her father's change of feeling. She sat down on the floor, as she had a way of doing, all in a little heap, staring at the empty grate. The fire had burnt out, and no one had thought of relighting it. For a few minutes her tears overflowed, and she cried and cried in two rivulets down her black little face. She thought how forlorn she was, what a dull life she lead, how alone she lived; such a rush of regret and misery overpowered her, that she hid her face in her hands, unconscious of anything else but her own sadness. . . .

She did not hear the bell ring, nor a carriage stop, nor Lady Jane's footsteps. She came across the room and stood looking at her. "Why, my dear little creature, what is the matter?" said the old lady at last. "Crying? don't you know it is very naughty to cry, no matter how bad things are? Are they all gone — are you all alone?"

Ella jumped up, quite startled, blushed, wiped her tears in a smudge. "I thought nobody would see me cry," she said, "for they are all gone to the Crystal Palace."

"And did they leave you behind quite by yourself?" the old lady asked.

"They were so sorry they had no room for me," said good-natured little Ella. She could not bear to hear people blamed. "They had promised Madame de Bricabrac."

"Is that all?" said Lady Jane, in her kind, imperious way. "Why, I have driven in from Hampstead on purpose to go there too. There's a great flower-show to-day, and you know I am a first-rate gardener. I've brought up a great hamper of things. Put on your bonnet, wash your face, and come along directly. I've plenty of room. Who is that talking in that rude way?" for at that instant Carter called out from the drawing-room door,—

"Now then, Miss Ella, you can come and help me fold them dresses. I'm in a hurry."

Carter was much discomposed when Lady Jane appeared, irate, dignified.

"Go upstairs directly, and do not forget yourself again," said the old lady.

"Oh, I think I ought to go and fold up the dresses!" said Ella, hesitating, flushing, blushing, and looking more than grateful. "How very, very kind of you to think of me! I'm afraid they wouldn't — I'm afraid I have no bonnet. Oh, thank you, I — but — "

"Nonsense, child," said Lady Jane; "my maid shall help that woman. Here," ringing the bell violently, to the footman,— "what have you done with the hamper I brought up? Let me see it unpacked here immediately. Can't trust those people, my dear, — always see to everything myself."

All sorts of delicious things, scents, colors, spring-flowers, and vegetables came out of the hamper in delightful confusion. It was a hamper full of treasures,— sweet, bright, delicious-tasted,— asparagus, daffodillies, bluebells, salads, cauliflowers, hothouse flowers, cowslips from the fields. azalias. Ella's natty little fingers arranged them all about the room in plates and in vases so perfectly and so quickly, that old Lady Jane cried out in admiration,—

"Why, you would be a first-rate girl, if you didn't cry. Here, you John, get some bowls and trays for the vegetables, green peas, strawberries; and oh, here's a cucumber and a nice little early pumpkin! I had it forced, my dear. Your stepmother tells me she is passionately fond of pumpkins. Here, John, take all this down to the cook; tell her to put it in a cool larder, and order the carriage and horses round directly. Now then," to Ella, briskly, "go and put your things on, and come along with me. I'll make matters straight. I always do. There, go directly. I can't have the horses kept. Raton, my coachman, is terrible if he is kept waiting, — frightens me to death by his driving when he is put out."

Ella did not hesitate a moment longer; she rushed upstairs; her little feet flew as they used to do formerly. She came down in a minute, panting, rapturous, with shining hair and a bright face, in her very best Sunday frock, cloak, and hat. Shabby enough they were, but she was too happy, too excited, to think about the deficiencies in her toilet.

"Dear me, this will never do, I see," said the old lady, looking at her disapprovingly; but she smiled so kindly as she spoke, that Ella was not a bit frightened.

"Indeed, I have no other," she said.

"John," cried the old lady, " where is my maid? Desire her to come and speak to me directly. Now then, sir ! "

All her servants knew her ways much too well not to fly at her commands.' A maid appeared as if by magic.

"Now, Batter, be quick; get that blue and silver bernouse of mine from the box upstairs,— it will look very nice; and a pair of gray kid gloves, Batter; and let me see, my dear, you wouldn't look well in a brocade. No, that gray satin skirt, Batter; her own white bodice will do, and we can buy a bonnet as we go along. Now, quick; am I to be kept waiting all day? "

Ella in a moment found herself transformed somehow into the most magnificent lady she had seen for many a day. It was like a dream, she could hardly believe it; she saw herself move majestically, sweeping in silken robes across the very same pier-glass, where ·a few minutes before she had looked at the wretched little, melancholy creature, crying with a dirty face, and watched the sad tears flowing. . . .

.   .   .   .

"Now then—now then," cried Lady Jane, who was always saying "Now then," and urging people on,— "where's my page —are the outriders there? They are all workhouse boys, my dear; they come to me as thin and starved as church mice, and then I fatten them up and get 'em situations. I always go with outriders. One's obliged to keep up a certain dignity in these Chartist days — universal reform — suffrage — vote by ballot. I've no patience with Mr. Gladstone, and it all rests with us to keep ourselves well aloof. Get in, get in! Drive to Sydenham, if you please."

Lady Jane's manners entirely changed when she spoke to Raton. And it is a fact that coachmen from their tall boxes rule with a very high hand, and most ladies tremble before them. Raton looked very alarming in his wig, with his shoe-buckles and great red face.

What a fairy tale it was ! There was little Ella sitting in this lovely chariot, galloping down the Brompton Road, with all the little boys cheering and hurrahing; and the little outriders clattering on ahead, and the old lady sitting bolt upright as pleased as Punch. She really *had* been going to Sydenham; but I think if she had not, she would have set off instantly, if she thought she would make anybody happy by so doing. They stopped at a shop in the Brompton Road — the wondering shop-woman came out.

"A white bonnet, if you please," said Lady Jane. "That will do very well. Here, child, put it on, and mind you don't crease the strings." And then away and away they went once more through the town, the squares, over the bridges. They saw the ships and steamers coming down the silver Thames, but the carriage never stopped : the outriders paid the tolls and clattered on ahead. They rolled along pleasant country lanes and fields, villas and country-houses, road-side inns and pedestrians, and crawling carts and carriages. At the end of three-quarters of an hour, during which it seemed to Ella as if the whole gay *cortège* had been flying through the air, they suddenly stopped at last, at the great gates of a Crystal Palace blazing in the sun and standing on a hill. A crowd was looking on. All sorts of grand people were driving up in their carriages; splendid ladies were passing in. Two gentlemen in white waistcoats were dismounting from their horses just·as Ella and Lady Jane were arriving. They rushed up to the carriage-door, and helped them to the ground.

"And pray, sir, who are you? " said Lady Jane, as soon as she was safely deposited on her two little flat feet, with the funny old-fashioned shoes.

The young man colored up and bowed. "You don't remember me, Lady Jane," he said. "Charles Richardson — I have had the honor of meeting you at Ash Place, and at Cliffe, my uncle's house. This is my friend Mr. Prettyman."

"This is Mr. Richardson, my dear Ella, and that is Mr. Prettyman. Tell them to come back in a couple of hours" (to the page), "and desire Raton to see that the horses have a feed. Now then — yes — give her your arm, and you are going to take me? — very well," to the other white waistcoat; and so they went into the palace.

What are young princes like nowadays? Do they wear diamond aigrettes, swords at their sides, top-boots, and little short cloaks over one shoulder? The only approach to romance that I can see is the flower in their button-hole, and the nice little mustaches and curly beards in which they delight. But all the same besides the flower in the button, there is also, I think, a possible flower of sentiment still growing in the soft hearts of princes in these days, as in the old days long, long ago.

Charles Richardson was a short, ugly little man, very gentleman-like, and well dressed. He was the next heir to a baronetcy; he had a pale face and a snub nose, and such a fine estate in prospect, — Cliffe Court its name was, — that I do not wonder at Miss Lisette's admiration for him. As for Ella, she thought how kind he had been on the stairs that morning; she thought what a bright, genial smile he had. How charming he looked! she said to herself; no, never, never, had she dreamed of any one so nice. She was quite — more than satisfied; no prince in romance would have seemed to her what this one was, there actually walking beside her. As for Richardson himself, it was a case of love at first sight. He had seen many thousand young ladies in the last few years, but not one of them to compare with this sweet-faced, ingenuous, tender, bright little creature. He offered her his arm, and led her along.

Ella observed that he said a few words to his friend; she little guessed their purport. "You go first," he whispered, "and if you see the Ashfords, get out of the way. I should have to walk with those girls, and my heart is here transfixed forever." . . "Where have I seen you before?" he went on, talking to Ella, as they roamed through the beautiful courts and gardens, among fountains and flowers, and rare objects of art. "Forgive me for asking you, but I must have met you somewhere long ago, and have never forgotten you. I am haunted by your face." Ella was too much ashamed to tell him where and how it was they had met that very morning. She remembered him perfectly, but she thought he would rush away and leave her, if she told him that the untidy little scrub upon the stairs had been herself. And she was so happy; music playing, flowers blooming, the great wonderful fairy palace, flashing over head; the kind, clever, delightful young man to escort her; the gay company, the glitter, the perfume, the statues, the interesting figures of Indians, the dear, dear, kind Lady Jane to look to for sympathy and for good-humored little nods of encouragement. She had never been so happy; she had never known what a wonder the palace might be. Her heart was so full. It was all so lovely, so inconceivably beautiful and delightful, that she was nearly tipsy with delight; her head turned for an instant, and she clung to young Richardson's protecting arm.

"Are you faint — are you ill?" he said, anxiously.

"Oh, no!" said Ella; "it's only that everything is so beautiful; it is almost more than I can bear. I — I am not often so happy; oh, it is so charming! I do not think anything could be so delightful in all the world." She looked herself so charming and unconscious as she spoke, looking up with her beautiful face out of her white bonnet, that the young fellow felt as if he must propose to her, then and there, offhand, on the very spot; and at the instant he looked up passionately — O horror! — he caught sight of the Ashfords, mother, daughters, Madame de Bricabrac, all in a row, coming right down upon them.

"Prettyman, this way to the right," cried little Richardson, desperately: and Prettyman, who was a good-natured fellow, said, "This way, please, Lady Jane; there's some people we want to avoid over there."

.   .   .   .

"I'm sure it was," Lisette said. "I knew the color of his waistcoat. Who could he have been walking with, I wonder?"

"Some lady of rank, evidently," said Julia. "I think they went up into the gallery in search of us."

"Let us go into the gallery, dears," said Mrs. Ashford, and away they trudged.

.   .   .   .

The young men and their companions had gone into the Tropics, and meanwhile were sitting under a spreading palm-tree, eating pink ices; while the music played and played more delightfully, and all the air was full of flowers and waltzes, of delight, of sentiment. To young Richardson the whole palace was Ella in everything, in every sound, and flower, and fountain; to Ella, young Richardson seemed an enormous giant, and his kind little twinkling eyes were shining all round her.

Poor dear! she was so little used to being happy, her happiness almost overpowered her.

"Are you going to the ball at Guildhall,

to-morrow?" Mr. Richardson was saying to his unknown princess. "How shall I ever meet you again? will you not tell me your name? But—"

"I wonder what o'clock it is, and where your mother can be, Ella," said Lady Jane. "It's very odd we have not met."

. . . .

"I can't imagine where they can have hid themselves," said Julia, very crossly, from the gallery overhead.

"I'm so tired, and I'm ready to drop," said Miss Lisette.

"Oh, let us sit," groaned Madame de Brica-brac. "I can walk no more; what does it matter if we do not find your friends?"

"If we take our places at the door," said Lisette, "we shall be sure to catch them as they pass."

. . . .

"Perhaps I may be able to go to the ball," said the princess, doubtfully. "I—I don't know." Lady Jane made believe not to be listening. The voices in the gallery passed on. Lady Jane having finished her ice, pulled out her little watch, and gave a scream of terror. "Heavens! my time is up," she said. "Raton will frighten me out of my wits, driving home. Come, child, come—come—come. Make haste—thank these gentlemen for their escort," and she went skurrying along, a funny little active figure, followed by the breathless young people. They got to the door at last, where Raton was waiting, looking very ferocious. "Oh, good-by," said Ella. "Thank you so much," as Richardson helped her into the chariot.

"And you will not forget me?" he said, in a low voice. "I shall not need any name to remember you by."

"My name is Ella," she answered, blushing, and driving off; and then Ella flung her arms round Lady Jane, and began to cry again, and said, "Oh, I have been so happy! so happy! How good, good of you to make me so happy! Oh, thank you, dear Lady Jane!"

The others came back an hour after them, looking extremely cross, and were much surprised to find Lady Jane in the drawing-room. "I am not going back till Wednesday," said the old lady, "I've several things to do in town. . . . Well, have you had a pleasant day?"

"Not at all," said Mrs. Ashford, plaintively. "The colonel deserted us; we didn't find our young men till just as we were coming away. We are all very tired,

and want some supper. Some of your delicious fruit, Lady Jane."

"Oh, dear, how tired I am!" said Julia.

"Poor Richardson was in very bad spirits," said Lisette.

"What a place it is for losing one another," said old Lady Jane. "I took Ella there this afternoon, and though I looked about I couldn't see you anywhere."

"*Ella!*" cried the other girls, astonished; "was *she* there?" . . . But they were too much afraid of Lady Jane to object more openly.

That evening, after the others left the room, as Ella was pouring out the tea, she summoned up courage to ask whether she might go to the ball at Guildhall with the others next evening. "Pray, pray, please take me," she implored. Mrs. Ashford looked up amazed at her audacity. Poor little Ella! refused, scorned, snubbed, wounded, pained, and disappointed. She finished pouring out the tea in silence, while a few bitter, scalding tears dropped from her eyes into the teacups. Colonel Ashford drank some of them, and asked for more sugar to put into his cup.

"There, never mind," he said, kindly. He felt vexed with his wife, and sorry for the child; but he was, as usual, too weak to interfere. "You know you are too young to go into the world, Ella. When your sisters are married, then *your* turn will come."

Alas! would it ever come? The day's delight had given her a longing for more; and now she felt the beautiful, glittering vision was only a vision, and over already: the cloud-capped towers, the gorgeous palace; and the charming prince himself,—was he a vision too? Ah! it was too sad to think of. Presently Lisette and Julia came back: they had been upstairs to see about their dresses.

"I shall wear my bird-of-paradise, and my yellow tarlatane," said Lisette; "gold and purple is such a lovely contrast."

"Gobert has sent me a lovely thing," said Julia; "tricolor flounces all the way up—she has so much taste."

Good old Lady Jane asked her maid next morning if any dress was being got ready for Miss Ella. Hearing that she was not going, and that no preparations were being made, she despatched Batter on a secret mission, and ordered her carriage at nine o'clock that evening. She went out herself soon after breakfast in a hired brougham, dispensing with the outriders for once.

Ella was hard at work all day for her sisters: her little fingers quilled, fluted, frilled, pleated, pinned, tacked the trimmings on their dresses more dexterously than any dressmaker or maid-servant could do. She looked so pretty, so kind, and so tired, so wistful, as she came to help them to dress, that Lisette was quite touched and said, — "Well, Ella, I shouldn't wonder if, after I am snapped up, you were to get hold of a husband some day. I dare say *some* people might think you nice-looking."

"Oh, do you think so really, Lisette?" said Ella, quite pleased; and then faltering, "Do you think . . . . Shall you see Mr. Richardson?"

"Of course I shall," said Lisette. "He was talking great nonsense yesterday after we found him; saying that he had met with perfection at last — very devoted altogether; scarcely spoke to me at all; but that is the greatest proof of devotion, you know. I know what he meant very well. I shouldn't be at all surprised if he was to propose to-night. I don't know whether I shall have him. I'm always afraid of being thrown away," said Lisette, looking over her shoulder at her train.

Ella longed to send a message, a greeting of some sort, to Lisette's adorer. Oh, how she envied her! what would she not have given to be going too? . . . .

"What! are not you dressing, child?" said Lady Jane, coming into the room. "Are they again obliged to call for Madame de Bricabrac? I had looked up a pair of shoe-buckles for you in case you went; but keep them all the same; they only want a little rubbing up."

"Oh, thank you; how pretty they are! how kind you are to me!" said Ella, sadly. "I — I — am not going." And she burst out crying.

It was just dreadful not to go; the poor child had had a great draught of delight the day before, and she was aching and sickening for more, and longing with a passion of longing which is only known to very young people — she looked quite worn and pale through her tears.

"Rub up your shoe-buckles, — that will distract you," said the old lady, kindly. "They are worth a great deal of money, though they are only paste; and if you peep in my room you will find a little pair of slippers to wear them with. I hope they will fit. I could hardly get any small enough for you." They were the loveliest little white satin slippers, with satin heels,

all embroidered with glass beads; but small as they were, they were a little loose, only Ella took care not to say so, as she tried them on.

We all know what is coming, though little Ella had no idea of it. The ball was at Guildhall, one of the grandest and gayest that ever was given in the city of London. It was in honor of the beautiful young Princess who had just landed on our shores. Princes, ambassadors, nobles, stars, orders and garters and decorations, were to be present; all the grandest, gayest, richest, happiest people in the country, all the most beautiful ladies and jewels and flowers, were to be there to do homage to the peerless young bride. The Ashfords had no sooner started, than Lady Jane, who had been very mysterious all day, and never told any one that she had been to the city to procure two enormous golden tickets which were up in her bedroom, now came, smiling very benevolently, into the drawing-room. Little Ella was standing out in the balcony with her pale face and all her hair tumbling down her back. She had been too busy to put it up, and now she was only thinking of the ball, and picturing the dear little, ugly, disappointed face of Prince Richardson, when he should look about everywhere for her in vain, while she was standing hopelessly gazing after the receding carriage.

"Well, my dear, have you rubbed up the shoe-buckles? That is right," said the old lady. "Now come quick into my room and see some of my conjuring."

Conjuring! It was the most beautiful white net dress, frothed and frothed up to the waist, and looped up with long grasses. The conjuring was her own dear old pearl necklace with the diamond clasp, and a diamond star for her hair. It was a bunch of grasses and delicate white azalias for a head-dress, and over all the froth a great veil of flowing white net. The child opened her violet eyes, gasped, screamed, and began dancing about the room like a mad thing, jumping, bounding, clapping her hands, all so softly and gayly, and yet so lightly, in such an ecstasy of delight, that Lady Jane felt she was more than rewarded.

.   .   .   .

"Ah! there she is at last!" cried Mr. Richardson, who was turning carefully round and round with the energetic Lisette. "What do you mean?" said Lisette.

Can you fancy her amazement when she looked round and saw Ella appearing in her

snow and sunlight dress, looking so beautiful that everybody turned to wonder at her
and to admire? As for Ella, she saw no
one, nothing, — she was looking up and
down, and right and left, for the kind little
pale plain face which she wanted.

"Excuse me one minute, Miss Lisette,"
said Mr. Richardson, leaving poor Lisette
planted in the middle of the room, and rushing forward.

"Are you engaged," Ella heard a breathless voice saying in her ear, "for the next
three, six, twenty dances? I am so delighted you have come! I thought you
were never coming."

Julia had no partner at all, and was standing close by the entrance with her mother.
They were both astounded at the appari-
tion. Mrs. Ashford came forward to make
sure that her eyes were not deceiving her.
Could it be? Yes, — no, — yes, it was Ella.
She flicked her fan indignantly into an al-
derman's eye, and looked so fierce that the
child began to tremble.

"Please forgive me, mamma," said Ella,
piteously.

"Forgive you! never," said Mrs. Ashford,
indignant. "What does all this mean,
pray?" she continued. "Lady Jane, I really
must — " and then she stopped, partly because she was so angry she could scarcely
speak, and partly because she could not
afford to quarrel with Lady Jane until the
season was over.

"You really must forgive me, dear Lydia,"
said Lady Jane. "She wanted to come so
much, I could not resist bringing her."

Weber's inspiriting last waltz was being
played. The people and music went waving to and fro like the waves of the sea;
sudden sharp notes of exceeding sweetness
sounded, and, at the sound, the figures all
swayed in harmony. The feet kept unseen
measure to the music; the harmonious
rhythm thrilled and controlled them all.
The music was like an enchantment, which
kept them moving and swaying in circles,
and in delightful subjection. Lassitude,
sadness, disappointment, Ella's alarm, — all
melted away for the time; pulses beat, and
the dancers seesawed to the measure.

All that evening, young Richardson
danced with Ella, and with no one else.
They scarcely knew how the time went.
It was a fairy world. They were flying and
swimming in melody, — the fairy hours
went by to music, in light, delightful com-
panionship. Ella did not care for. Mrs.
Ashford's darkening looks, for anything

that might happen; she was so happy in
the moment, she almost forgot to look for
Lady Jane's sympathetic glance.

"You must meet me in the ladies' cloak-
room, punctually at half-past eleven," her
patroness had whispered to her. "I cannot keep Raton, with his bad cough, out
after twelve o'clock. Mind you are punctual, for I have promised not to keep him
waiting."

"Yes, yes, dear Lady Jane,"said Ella; and
away she danced again to the music. And
time went on, and Julia had no partners;
and Colonel Ashford came up to his wife,
saying, "I'm so glad you arranged for Ella
too. How nice she is looking! What is the
matter with Julia; why don't she dance?"
Tumty, tumty, tumty, went the instruments. And meanwhile Mr. Richardson
was saying, "Your dancing puts me in
mind of a fairy I once saw in a field at Cliffe
long ago. Nobody would ever believe me,
but I did see one."

"A fairy! what was she like?" asked
Ella.

"She was very like you," said Mr. Richardson, laughing. "I do believe it was you, and
that was the time when I saw you before."

"No, it was not," said Ella, blushing, and
feeling she ought to confess. "I will tell
you," she said, "if you will promise to
dance one more dance with me, after you
know. Only one."

"Then you, too, remember," he cried,
eagerly. "One more dance? Twenty, —
forever and ever. Ah, you must know, you
must guess the feeling in my heart!"

.   .   .   .

"Listen, first," said Ella, trembling very
much, and waltzing on very slowly. "It
was only the other day — " The clock
struck three-quarters.

"Ella, I am going," said Lady Jane, tap-
ping her on the shoulder. "Come along,
my dear."

"One word!" cried Richardson, eagerly.

"You can stay with your mother if you
like," the old lady went on, preoccupied, —
she was thinking of her coachman's ire;
"but I advise you to come with me."

"Oh, pray, pray stay!" said young Richardson. "Where is your mother? Let me
go and ask her!"

"You had better go yourself, Ella," said
old Lady Jane. "Will you give me your
arm to the door, Mr. Richardson?"

Ella went up to Mrs. Ashford — she was
bold with happiness to-night — and made
her request. "Stay with me? certainly

not; it is quite out of the question. You do me great honor," said the lady, laughing sarcastically. "Lady Jane brought you, Lady Jane must take you back," said the step-mother. "Follow your chaperone if you please; I have no room for you in my brougham. Go directly, miss!" said Mrs. Ashford, so savagely that the poor child was quite frightened, and set off running after the other two. She would have caught them up, but at that instant, Lisette — who had at last secured a partner — came waltzing up in such a violent, angry way, that she bumped right up against the little flying maiden, and nearly knocked her down. Ella gave a low cry of pain. They had trodden on her foot roughly; they had wounded her; her little satin slipper had come off. Poor Ella stooped and tried to pull at the slipper, but other couples came surging up, and she was alone, and frightened, and obliged to shuffle a little way out of the crowd before she could get it on. The poor little frightened thing thought she never should get through the crowd. She made the best of her way to the cloak-room, — it seemed to her as if she had been hours getting there. At last she reached it, only to see, to her dismay, as she went in at one door, the other two going out of another a long way off! She called, but they did not hear her; and at the same moment St. Paul's great clock began slowly to strike twelve. "My cloak, my cloak, — anything, please," she cried in great agitation and anxiety; and a stupid, bewildered maid hastily threw a shabby old shawl over her shoulders, — it belonged to some assistant in the place. Little Ella, more and more frightened, pulled it up as she hurried along the blocked passages and corridors all lined with red and thronged with people. They all stared at her in surprise as she flew along. Presently her net tunic caught in a doorway and tore into a long ragged shred which trailed after her. In her agitation her comb fell out of her hair, — she looked all scared and frightened, — nobody would have recognized the beautiful triumphal princess of half an hour before. She heard the linkmen calling, "Peppercorne's carriage stops the way!" and she hurried faster and faster down the endless passages and steps, and at last, just as she got to the doorway, — O horror! she saw the carriage and outriders going gleaming off in the moonlight, while everything else looked black, dark, and terrible.

"Stop, stop, please stop!" cried little Ella, rushing out into the street through the amazed footmen and linkmen. "Stop! stop!" she cried, flying past Richardson himself, who could hardly believe his eyes. Raton only whipped his horses, and Ella saw them disappearing into gloom in the distance in a sort of agony of despair. She was excited beyond measure, and exaggerated all her feelings. What was to be done? Go back? That was impossible. Walk home? She did not know her way. Was it fancy? — was not somebody following her? She felt quite desperate in the moonlight and darkness. At that instant it seemed to her like a fairy chariot coming to her rescue, when a cabman, who was slowly passing, stopped and said, "Cab, mum?"

"Yes! oh, yes! To Onslow Square!" cried Ella, jumping in and shutting the door in delight and relief. She drove off just as the bewildered little Richardson, who had followed her, reached the spot. He came up in time only to see the cab drive off, and to pick up something which was lying shining on the pavement. It was one of the diamond buckles which had fallen from her shoe as she jumped in. This little diamond buckle might, perhaps, have led to her identification, if young Richardson had not taken the precaution of ascertaining from old Lady Jane, Ella's name and address.

He sent a servant next morning with a little parcel, and a note to inquire whether one of the ladies had lost what was enclosed, and whether Colonel Ashford would see him at one o'clock on business.

"Dear me, what a pretty little buckle!" said Lisette, trying it on her large, flat foot. "It looks very nice, don't it, Julia? I think I guess — don't you? — what he is coming for. I shall say 'No.'"

"It's too small for you. It would do better for me," said Julia, contemplating her own long slipper, embellished with the diamonds. "It is not ours. We must send it back, I suppose."

"A shoebuckle," said Ella, coming in from the kitchen, where she had been superintending preserves in her little brown frock. "Let me see it. Oh, how glad I am! it is mine. Look here!" and she pulled the fellow out of her pocket. "Lady Jane gave them to me."

And so the prince arrived before luncheon, and was closeted with Colonel Ashford, who gladly gave his consent to what he wanted. And when Mrs. Ashford began to explain things to him, as was her way, he did not listen to a single word she said. He was so absorbed wondering when Ella was coming into the room. He thought once he heard a little rustle on the stairs outside, and he jumped up and rushed to the door. It was Ella, sure enough, in her shabby little gown. Then he knew where and when he had seen her before.

"Ella, why did you run away from me last night?" he said. "You see I have followed you after all."

8

They were so good, so happy, so devoted to one another, that even Lisette and Julia relented. Dear little couple! good luck go with them, happiness, content, and plenty. There was something quite touching in their youth, tenderness, and simplicity, and, as they drove off in their carriage for the honeymoon, Lady Jane flung the very identical satin slipper after them which Ella should have lost at the ball.

LITTLE RED RIDING HOOD.

BY

MISS THACKERAY,

AUTHOR OF "BEAUTY AND THE BEAST."

———

LORING, Publisher,

319 WASHINGTON STREET,

BOSTON.

1867.

LITTLE RED RIDING HOOD.

I.

THERE is something sad in most pretty stories, in most lovely strains, in the tenderest affections and friendships; but tragedy is a different thing from the indefinable feeling which lifts us beyond to-day, into that dear and happy region where our dearest loves, and plays, and dreams are to be found even in childish times. Poor little Red Riding Hood, with bright eyes glancing from her scarlet caplet, has been mourned by generations of children; but though they pity her, and lament her sad fate, she is no familiar playmate and companion. That terrible wolf with the fiery eyes, glaring through the brushwood, haunts them from the very beginning of the story; — it is too sad, too horrible, and they hastily turn the leaves and fly to other and better loved companions, with whose troubles they sympathize, for they are but passing woes, and they know that brighter times are in store. For the poor little maiden at the well, for dear Cinderella, for Roe-brother and little sister, wandering through the glades of the forest, and Snowwhite and her sylvan court of kindly woodland dwarfs, — all these belong to the sweet and gentle region where beautiful, calm suns shine after the storm, amid fair landscapes, and gardens, and palaces. Even we elders sympathize with the children in this feeling, although we are more or less hardened by time, and have ourselves, wandering in the midway of life, met with wolves roving through the forest, — wolves from whose cruel claws, alas! no father's or mother's love can protect us, and against whose wiles all warnings except those of our own experience are vain. And these wolves devour little boys as well as little girls and pats of butter.

This is no place to write of some stories, so sad and so hopeless that they can scarcely be spoken; although good old Perrault, in his simple way, to some poor Red Riding Hoods straying from the path, utters a word of warning rhyme at the end of the old French edition. Some stories are too sad; others too trifling. The sketch which I have in my mind is no terrible tragedy, but a silly little tale, so foolish and trivial that if it were not that it comes in its place with the others, I should scarcely attempt to repeat it. I met all the personages by chance at Fontainebleau only the other day.

The wolf was playing the fiddle under Little Red Riding Hood's window. Little Red Riding Hood was peeping from behind her cotton curtains. Rémy (that was the wolf's Christian name) could see the little balls bobbing, and guessed that she was there. He played on louder than ever, dragging his bow with long, sobbing chords across his fiddle-strings, and as he played a fairy palace arose at his bidding, more beautiful than the real old palace across the Place that we had come to see. The fairy palace arose story upon story, lovely to look upon, enchanted, — a palace of art, with galleries, and terraces, and belvederes, and orange-flowers scenting the air, and fragrant blossoms falling in snow-showers, and fountains of life murmuring and turning marble to gold as they flowed. Red Riding Hood from behind her cotton curtains, and Rémy, her cousin, outside in the court-yard, were the only two inhabitants of this wonderful building. They were alone in it together, far away in that world of which I have been speaking, at a long, long distance from the every-day all round about them, though the cook of the hotel was standing at his kitchen-door, and the stable-boy was grinning at Rémy's elbow, and H. and I, who had arrived only that evening, were sitting resting on the bench in front of the hotel, among the autumnal profusion of nasturtiums and marigolds with which the court-yard was planted. H. and I had come to see the palace, and to walk about in the stately old gardens, and to breathe a little quiet and silence after the noise of the machines thundering all day in the Great Ex-

8

hibition of the Champ de Mars, the din of
the cannons firing, of the carriages and multitudes rolling along the streets.

The Maynards, Red Riding Hood's parents, were not passers-by like ourselves;
they were comfortably installed at the hotel
for a month at a time, and came over once
a year to see Mrs. Maynard's mother, an old
lady who had lived at Fontainebleau as long
as her two daughters could remember. This
old lady's name was Madame Capuchon;
but her first husband had been an English-
man, like Mr. Maynard, her son-in-law, who
was also her nephew by this first marriage.
Both Madame Capuchon's daughters were
married, — Marthe, the eldest, to Henry
Maynard, an English country gentleman:
Félicie, the youngest, to the Baron de la
Louvière, who resided at Poictiers and who
was sous-préfet there.

It is now nearly forty years since Madame
Capuchon first went to live at Fontainebleau, in the old house at the corner of the
Rue de la Lampe. It has long been doomed
to destruction, with its picturesque high
roof, its narrow windows and balconies and
sunny old brick passages and staircases, with
the round ivy œil-de-bœuf windows. Staircases were piled up of brick in the time of
the Louises, broad and wide, and easy to
climb, and not of polished wood, like the
slippery flights of to-day. However, the old
house is in the way of a row of shops and
a projected café and newspaper office; so
are the ivy-grown garden-walls, the acacia-
trees, the sun-dial, and the old stone seat.
It is a pity that newer buildings cannot
sometimes be selected for destruction; they
might be rebuilt and redestroyed again and
again, and people who care for such things
might be left in peace a little longer to hold
the dear old homes and traditions of their
youth.

Madame Capuchon, however, is a kind
and despotic old lady; she has great influence and authority in the town, and during
her life the old house is safe. It is now, as
I have said, forty years since she first came
to live there, — a young widow for the second time, with two little daughters and a
faithful old maid to be her only companions
in her flight from the world where she had
known great troubles and changes. Madame Capuchon and her children inhabited
the two upper stories of the old house. The
rez de chaussée was partly a porter's lodge,
partly a warehouse, and partly a little apartment which the proprietor reserved for his
use. He died twice during Madame Capu-

chon's tenancy; once he ventured to propose to her, — but this was the former owner
of the place, not the present proprietor,
an old bachelor who preferred his Paris café
and his boulevard to the stately silence and
basking life of Fontainebleau.

This life suited Madame Capuchon, who
from sorrow at first, and then from habit,
continued the same silent cloistered existence for years, — years which went by and
separated her quietly but completely from
her old habits and friends and connections
and long-past troubles, while the little girls
grew up and the mother's beauty changed,
faded quietly away in the twilight life she
was leading.

The proprietor who had ventured to propose to the widow, and who had been
refused with so much grace and decision
that his admiration remained unaltered, was
no more; but shortly before his death he
had a second time accosted her with nego-
tiations of marriage, — not for himself this
time, but for a nephew of his, the Baron de
la Louvière, who had seen the young ladies
by chance, heard much good of them from
his uncle and their attached attendant Simonne, and learned that their dot was ample
and their connections respectable. Marthe,
the eldest daughter, was the least good-
looking of the two, but to most people's
mind far more charming than Félicie, the
second. M. de la Louvière had at first sight
a slight preference for Marthe, but learning through his uncle that an alliance was
contemplated between her and an English
connection of her mother's, he announced
himself equally anxious to obtain the hand
of Félicie, the younger sister. After some
hesitation, much addition of figures, sub-
traction, division, rule of three worked out,
consultations and talk between Simonne and
her mistress, and long discussions with
Henry Maynard himself, who was staying
with a friend at Fontainebleau at the time,
this favor was accorded to the baron.

The young baroness went off nothing
loth; she was bored at home, she did not
like the habit of severity and silence into
which her mother had fallen. She was a
slim, active, decided person, of calm affections, but passionately fond of her own way,
as indeed was Madame Capuchon herself,
for all her regrets for that past in which it
must be confessed she had always done exactly as she liked, and completely ruled her
two husbands. For all Madame Capuchon's
blacks and drabs and seclusion, and shut
shutters, and confessors, and shakes of the

head, she had greatly cheered up by this time; she had discovered in her health a delightful source of interest and amusement. Félicie's marriage was as good as a play, as the saying goes; and then came a catastrophe, still more exciting than Félicie's brilliant prospects, which occupied all the spare moments of the two years which succeeded the youngest girl's departure from home.

Madame Capuchon's nephew, Henry Maynard, was, as I have said, staying at Fontainebleau with a friend, who was unfortunately a very good-looking young man of very good family, who had come to Fontainebleau to be out of harm's way, and to read French for some diplomatic appointment. Maynard used to talk to him about his devotion for his pretty cousin Marthe with the soft trill in her voice and the sweet, quick eyes. Young Lord John, alas! was easily converted to this creed, — he also took a desperate fancy to the pretty young lady; and Madame Capuchon, whose repeated losses had not destroyed a certain ambition which had always been in her nature, greatly encouraged the young man. And so one day poor Maynard was told that he must resign himself to his hard fate. He had never hoped much, for he knew well enough that his cousin, as he called her, did not care for him; Marthe had always discouraged him, although her mother would have scouted the notion that one of her daughters should resist any décree she might lay down, or venture to think for herself on such matters.

When Lord John proposed in the English fashion to Marthe one evening in the deep embrasure of the drawing-room window, Madame Capuchon was enchanted, although disapproving of the irregularity of the proceeding. She announced her intention of settling upon her eldest daughter a sum so large and so much out of the proportion to the dot which she had accorded to Madame de la Louvière, that the baron hearing of it by chance through Monsieur Micotton, the family solicitor, was furious, and an angry correspondence then commenced between him and his mother-in-law, which lasted many years, and in which Madame Capuchon found another fresh interest to attach her to life and an unfailing vent for much of her spare energy and excitement.

Henry Maynard went back to his father's house at Littleton on Thames, to console himself as best he could among the punts and the water-lilies. Lord John went back to England to pass his examination, and to gain his family's consent, without which he said he could not marry; and Marthe waited in the old house with Simonne and her mother, and that was the end of her story.

Lord John didn't pass his examination, but interest was made for him, and he was given another chance, and he got the diplomatic appointment all the same, and he went to Russia and was heard of no more at Fontainebleau. Madame Capuchon was naturally surprised at his silence; while Marthe wondered and wearied, but spoke no word of the pain which consumed her. Her mother sat down and wrote to the duke, presented her compliments, begged to remind him of his son's engagement, and requested information of the young man's whereabouts and intentions. In the course of a week she received a few polite lines from the duchess, regretting that she could give Madame Capuchon no information as to Lord John's whereabouts or intentions, informing her that she had made some mistake as to his engagement, and begged to decline any further correspondence on the subject, on paper so thick that Simonne had to pay double postage for the epistle, and it would scarcely burn when Madame Capuchon flung it into the fire. The widow stamped her little foot, flashed her eyes, bit her lips, darted off her compliments to the duchess a second time, and begged to inform her that her son was a coward and a false gentleman, and that it was the Capuchon family that now begged to decline any further communication with people who held their word so cheaply. Naturally enough, no answer came to this, although Madame Capuchon expected one, and fumed and flashed and scolded for weeks after, during which poor Marthe still wondered and knew nothing.

"Don't let us tell her anything about it," Simonne had said, when the first letter came. "Let her forget 'tout doucement,'" and Madame Capuchon agreed.

And so Marthe waited and forgot tout doucement, as Simonne proposed, for fifteen years, and the swans came sailing past her when she took her daily walk, and the leaves fell and grew again, and every night the shadow of the old lamp swinging in the street outside cast its quaint lines and glimmer across her dark, leaf-shaded room, and the trees rustled when the wind blew, and her dreams were stranger and less vivid.

Once Henry Maynard wrote soon after Lord John's desertion, renewing his propo-

. sals, to Marthe herself and not to his aunt; but the letter came too soon. And, indeed, it was by Henry Maynard's letter that Marthe first realized for certain what had happened.

But it came too soon. She could not yet bear to hear her faithless lover blamed. Lord John was a villain, and unworthy of a regret, Henry said. Would she not consent to accept an honest man instead of a false one?

"No, no, no, a hundred times no," cried Marthe to herself, with something of her mother's spirit, and she nervously wrote her answer and slid out by herself and posted it. She never dared tell Madame Capuchon what she had done.

As time went on, one or two other "offers" were made to her; but Marthe was so reluctant that as they were not very good ones Madame Capuchon let them go by, and then Marthe had a long illness, and then more time passed by.

"What have we been about?" said Madame Capuchon, to her confidante one day as her daughter left the room. "Here she is an old maid, and it is all her own obstinacy."

At thirty-three Marthe was still unmarried: a gracious, faded woman, who had caught the trick of being sad; although she had no real trouble, and had almost forgotten Lord John. But she had caught the trick of being sad, as I say, of flitting aimlessly across the rooms, of remembering and remembering instead of living for to-day.

Madame Capuchon was quite cheerful by this time; besides her health, her angry correspondence, her confessor, her game of dóminos, and her talks with Simonne, she had many little interests to fill up spare gaps and distract her when M. de la Louvière's demands were too much for her temper. There was her comfortable hot and well-served little dinner to look forward to, her paper to read of a night, her chocolate in bed every morning, on a nice little tray with a pat of fresh butter and her nice little new roll from the English baker's. Madame was friande, and Simonne's delight was to cater for her. But none of these distractions quite sufficed to give an interest to poor Marthe's sad life. She was too old for the fun and excitement of youth, and too young for the little comforts, the resignations and satisfactions of age. Simonne, the good old fat woman, used to think of her as a little girl, and try to devise new

treats for her as she had done when Félicie and Marthe were children. Marthe would kiss her old nurse gratefully, and think, with a regretful sigh, how it was that she could no longer be made happy by a bunch of flowers, a hot buttered cake, a new trimming to her apron: she would give the cake away to the porter's grandchildren, put the flowers into water and leave them, fold up the apron, and, to Simonne, most terrible sign of all, forget it in the drawer. It was not natural, — something must be done, thought the old woman.

The old woman thought and thought, and poked about, and one day, with her spectacles on her nose, deciphered a letter which was lying on Madame Capuchon's table; it was signed Henry Maynard, and announced the writer's arrival at Paris. Next day, when Simonne was frizzling her mistress's white curls (they had come out of their seclusion for some years past), she suddenly asked what had become of Monsieur Maynard, madame's English nephew, who used to come so often before Mademoiselle Félicie was married.

"What is that to you?" said the old lady. "He is at Paris. I heard from him yesterday."

"And why don't you ask him to come down and see you?" said Simonne, frizzling away at the crisp silver locks. "It would cheer mademoiselle to have some one to talk to. We don't want any one; we have had our day, you and I, but mademoiselle, I confess I don't like to see her going on as she does."

"Nor I," said the old lady, sharply. "She is no credit to me. One would almost think that she reproaches me for her existence, after all the sacrifices I have made."

Simonne went on frizzling without stopping to inquire what these sacrifices might be. "I will order a fricandeau for to-morrow," she said; "madame had better invite monsieur to spend the day."

"Simonne, you are an old fool," said her mistress. "I have already written to my nephew to invite him to my house."

Maynard came and partook of the fricandeau, and went for a little walk with Marthe, and he had a long talk with his aunt and old Simonne in the evening, and went away quite late, — past ten o'clock it was. Maynard did not go back to Paris that night, but slept at the hotel, and early next morning there came a note addressed to Marthe, in which the writer stated that he was still of the same mind in which he had been fifteen years before, and if she was of a different way of thinking, would she consent to accept him as her husband?

And so it came about that long after the first best hopes of her youth were over, Marthe consented to leave her own silent home for her husband's, a melancholy, middle-aged bride, sad and frightened at the thought of the tempestuous world into which she was being cast adrift, and less able at thirty-three than at twenty to hold her own against the kindly domineering old mother, who was much taken with the idea of this marriage, and vowed that Marthe should go, and that no daughter of hers should die an old maid if she could help it. She had been married twice herself; once at least, if possible, she was determined that both her daughters should follow her example. Félicie's choice was not all that Madame Capuchon could have wished as far as liberality and amiability of character were concerned, but Félicie herself was happy, and indeed — so Madame Capuchon had much reason to suspect — abetted her husband in his grasping and extortionate demands. " And now Marthe's turn had come," said Madame Capuchon, complacently, sitting among her pillows, sipping her chocolate; " she was the eldest, she should have married first; she had been a good and devoted daughter, she would make an excellent wife," cried the valiant old lady.

When Marthe demurred, " Go, my child, go in peace, only go, go, go. Simonne is quite able to take care of me: do you think I want the sacrifice of your life? For what should I keep you? Can you curl me, can you play at dominos? You are much more necessary to your cousin than you are to me. He will be here directly. What a figure you have made of yourself! Simonne, come here, give a coup de peigne to mademoiselle. There, I hear the bell; Henry will be waiting."

" He does not mind waiting, mamma," said Marthe, smiling sadly. " He has waited fifteen years already."

" So much the worse for you both," cried the old lady, angrily. " If I had only had my health, if my spirits had not been completely crushed in those days, I never would have given in to such ridiculous ideas."

Ridiculous ideas! This was all the epitaph that was uttered by any one of them over the grave where poor Marthe had buried with much pain and many tears the

trouble of her early life. She herself had no other text for the wasted love of her youth. How angry she had been with her cousin Henry when he warned her once; how she had hated him when he asked her to marry him before, tacitly forcing upon her the fact of his friend's infidelity; and now it was to Maynard after all that she was going to be married, — after all that had passed, all the varying fates, and loves, and hopes and expectations of her life! A sudden alarm came over the poor woman. Was she to leave it, this still life, and the old house, and the tranquil shade and silence, — and for what? Ah, she could not go, she could not; she would stay where she was. Ah! why would they not leave her alone?

Marthe went up to her room and cried, and bathed her eyes and cried again, and dabbed more water to dry her tears; then she came quietly down the old brick stairs. She passed along the tiled gallery, her slim figure reflecting in the dim old looking-glass in the alcove at the end, with the cupids engraved upon its mouldy surface. She hesitated a moment, and then took courage and opened the dining-room door. There was nobody there. It was all empty, dim-panelled, orderly, with its narrow tall windows reflecting the green without, and the gables and chimney-stacks piling under the blue. He was in the drawing-room then; she had hoped to find him here. Marthe sighed and then walked on across the polished floor, and so into the drawing-room. It was dimmer, more chill than the room in which their meals were served. Some one was standing waiting for her in one of the windows. Marthe remembered at that instant that it was Lord John's window; but she had little time for such reminiscences. A burly figure turned at her entrance, and Henry Maynard came to meet her, with one big hand out, and his broad, good-natured face beaming.

" Well, Minnie," said Henry Maynard, calling her by his old name for her, " you see I am here again already."

" Yes," she answered, standing before him, and then they were both silent; these two middle-aged people waiting for the other to speak.

" How is your mother?" Maynard asked. " I thought her very little changed; but you are not looking over well. However, time touches us all."

Marthe drew herself up, with her eyes gleaming in her pale face, and then there was another silence. At last Marthe faltered out, gaining courage as she went on, —

"I have been agitated, and a little disturbed. My mother is quite well, cousin Henry," she said; and as she spoke, her sad looks encountered Maynard's good-natured twinkling glance. She blushed suddenly like a girl of fifteen. "You seem amused," she said, with some annoyance.

"Yes, dear," spoke Maynard, in his kind, manly tones. "I am amused that you and I, at our time of life, should be shilly-shallying and sentimentalizing, like a couple of chits who have all their life before them, and don't care whether they know or not what is coming next. I want to know very much, — for I have little time to lose, — what do you and your mother think of my letter this morning?"

This was coming to the point very abruptly, Mademoiselle Capuchon thought.

"I am so taken by surprise," Marthe faltered, retreating a step or two, and nervously twisting her apron round about her fingers. "She wishes it. I — I hardly know. I have had so little time to —— "

"My dear Marthe," said Maynard, impatiently, "I am not a romantic young man. I can make no professions and speeches. You must take me as I am, if I suit you. I won't say that after you sent me away I have never thought of anybody but you during these past fifteen years. But we might have been very happy together all this long time, and yesterday when I saw how hipped you were looking, I determined to try and bring you away with me from this dismal place into the fresh air of Littleton, that is, if you liked to come with me of your own free will, and not only because my aunt desires it." And Henry Maynard drew a long breath, and put his hands in his pockets.

This honest little speech was like a revelation to Marthe. She had come down feeling like a victim, meaning graciously perhaps, in the end, to reward Maynard's constancy, taking it for granted that all this time he had never ceased being in love. She found that it was from old friendship and kindness alone that he had come to her again, not from sentiment, and yet this kindness and protection touched her more than any protestations of romantic affection.

"But — but — should you really like it?" she stammered, forgetting all her dreams, and coming to life, as it were, at that instant.

"Like it," he said, with a smile. "You don't know how fond I mean to be of you, if you will come with me, dear Marthe. You shall make me as happy as you like, and yourself into the bargain. I don't think you will be sorry for it, and indeed you don't seem to have been doing much good here, all by yourself. Well, is it to be yes or no?" And once more Maynard held out the broad brown hand.

And Marthe said, "Yes," quite cheerfully, and put her hand into his.

Marthe got to know her future husband better in these five minutes than in all the thirty years which had gone before.

The Maynards are an old Catholic family, so there were no difficulties on the score of religion. The little chapel in the big church was lighted up; the confessor performed the service. Madame Capuchon did not go, but Simonne was there in robes of splendor; and so were the De la Louvières. The baron and his mother-in-law had agreed to a temporary truce on this auspicious occasion. After the ceremony the new married pair went back to a refection which the English baker and Simonne had concocted between them. The baron and baroness had brought their little son Rémy, to whom they were devoted, and he presented Marthe with a wedding present — a large porcelain vase, upon which was a painting of his mother's performance, — in both his parents' name. Madame Capuchon brought out a lovely pearl and emerald necklace, which Félicie had coveted for years past.

"I must get it done up," the old lady said; "you won't want it immediately, Marthe; you shall have it the first time you come to see me. Do not delay too long," added Madame Capuchon, with a confidential shake of her head, to her son-in-law Maynard, as Marthe went away to change her dress. "You see my health is miserable. I am a perfect martyr. My doctor tells me my case is serious; not in so many words, but he assures me that he cannot find out what ails me, and when doctors say that, we all know what it means."

Henry Maynard attempted to reassure Madame Capuchon, and to induce her to take a more hopeful view of her state; but she grew quite angry and snapped him up so short with her immediate prospect of dissolution, that he desisted in his well-meant endeavors, and the old lady continued more complacently, —

"Do not be uneasy; if anything happens to me Simonne will write directly to your address. Do not forget to leave it with her. And now go and fetch your wife, and let me have the pleasure of seeing her in her travelling dress."

It was a kind old lady, but there was a want in her love; so it seemed to her son-in-law as he obeyed her behest. Marthe had never quite known what real love was, he thought. Sentiment, yes, and too much of it, but not that best home-love, — familiar, tender, unchanging. Her mother had not got it in her to give. Félicie de la Louvière was a hard and clear-headed woman; all her affection was for Rémy, her little boy. Maynard disliked her and the baron, too, but they were all apparently very good friends.

Marthe came back to the salle to say good-by, looking like herself again, Maynard thought, as his bride, in her rippling trailing, gray silks, entered the room, with Simonne's big bouquet of roses in her hand, and a pretty pink glow in her cheeks.

She was duly embraced by Félicie and her husband, and then she knelt down to ask for her mother's blessing. "Bless you! bless you!" cried Madame Capuchon, affectionately pushing her away. "There, you will disarrange yourself; take care, take care." Simonne sprang to the rescue, and Marthe found herself all at once embraced, stuck with pins, shaken out, tucked in, flattened, folded, embraced again; the handkerchief with which she had ventured to wipe her tears was torn out of her hand, folded, smoothed, and replaced. "Voilà!" said Simonne, with two last loud kisses, "bon voyage; good luck go with you." And Maynard following after, somewhat to his confusion, received a couple of like salutations.

———

II.

SIMONNE'S benediction followed Mrs. Maynard to England, where she went and took possession of her new home. The neighbors called; the drawing-room chintzes were renewed; Marthe Capuchon existed no longer; no one would have recognized the listless ghost flitting here and there, and gazing from the windows of the old house in the Rue de la Lampe, in the busy and practical mistress ·of Henry Maynard's home. She had gained in composure and spirits and happiness since she came to England. Her house was admirably administered; she wore handsome shining silk dresses and old lace; and she rustled and commanded as

efficiently as if she had been married for years. Simonne threw up her hands with delight at the transformation the first time she saw Marthe after her marriage. "But you are a hundred times better-looking than Madame la Baronne," said the old woman. "This is how I like to see you." The chief new blessing and happiness of all those blessings and happinesses which Simonne had wished to Marthe Maynard was a blessing called Marthe, too. It is considered a pretty name in French, and Maynard loved it for his wife's sake, and, as time went on, for her daughter's as well. He called her Patty, however, to distinguish the two. Far more than the happiness some people find in the early spring, in the voices of birds, the delight of the morning hours, the presence of this little thing brought to her mother, this bright, honest, black and brown and white and coral maiden, with her sweet and wilful ways. and gay, shrill warble. Every year the gay voice became more clear and decided, the ways more pretty and more wilful. Mrs. Maynard used to devise pretty, fanciful dresses for her Patty, and to tie bright ribbons in the child's crisp brown locks, and watch over her and pray for her from morning to night. 'Squire Maynard, who was a sensible man, used to be afraid lest so much affection should be bad for his little girl; he tried to be stern now and then, and certainly succeeded in frightening Patty on such occasions. The truth was, he loved his wife tenderly, and thought that Patty made a slave of her mother at times. It was a happy bondage for them both. Marthe dreamt no more dreams now, and only entered that serene country of her youth by proxy, as it were, and to make plans for her Patty. The child grew up as the years went by, but if Marthe made plans for her they were very distant ones, and to the mother as impossible still as when Patty had been a little baby tumbling in her cradle. Even then Marthe had settled that Patty was not to wait for years, as she had waited. What hero there was in the big world worthy of her darling, Mrs. Maynard did not know. The mother's heart sickened the first time she ever thought seriously of a vague possibility, of which the very notion filled her with alarm. She had a presentiment the first time that she ever saw him.

She was sitting alone in her bedroom, drowsily stitching in the sunlight of the pleasant bow-window, listening to the sound of the clippers at work upon the ivy-hedge close by, and to the distant chime from the clock-tower of the town across the river. Just below her window spread the lawn where her husband's beloved flower-beds were flushing, — scarlet and twinkling violet, white and brilliant amber. In the field beyond the sloping lawn some children were pulling at the sweet wild summer garlands hanging in the hedges, and the Alderneys were crunching through the long, damp grasses. Two pretty creatures had straggled down hill to the water-side, and were looking at their own brown eyes reflected in a chance clear pool in the margin of the river. For the carpet of green and meadow verdure was falling over, and lapping and draggling in the water in a fringe of glistening leaves and insects and weeds. There were white, creamy meadow-sweets, great beds of purple flowers, bronzed waterdocks, arching and crisping their stately heads, weeds up-springing, golden, slimy water-lilies floating upon their shining leaves. A water-rat was starting out of his hole, a dragon-fly floating along the bank. All this was at the foot of the sloping mead down by the bridge. It crossed the river to the little town of spires and red brick gables, which had been built about two centuries ago, and all round about spread hills and lawns and summer corn-fields. Marthe Maynard had seen the corn-fields ripen year after year; she loved the place for its own sake, and for the sake of those who were very dear to her then; but to-day, as she looked, she suddenly realized, poor soul, that a time might come when the heart and the sweetest life of this little home-Eden might go from it. And as she looked through her window something like a chill came over her: she dropped her work into her lap, and sat watching two figures climbing up the field side by side; coming through the buttercups, disappearing behind the hedge, reappearing at the bottom of the lawn, and then one figure darted forwards, while the other lingered a little among the flower-beds; and Mrs. Maynard got up resolutely, with a pain and odd apprehension in her heart, and went down to meet her daughter. The steeple of the little town, which strike the hours, half-hours, and the very minutes as they pass, were striking four quarters, and then five again, as Mrs. Maynard came out upon her lawn, and at each stroke the poor mother's heart sank, and she turned a little sick at the possibility which had first occurred to her just now in her own room. It seemed to thrust itself again upon her as she stood waiting

for the two young people, — her own Patty and the strange young man coming through the flower-beds.

There was a certain likeness to herself, odd, touching, bewildering, in the utter stranger, which said more plainly than any words, I belong to you and yours; I am no stranger, though strange to you. Patty had no need to explain, all breathless and excited and blushing, "Mamma, do you know who this is? This is Rémy de la Louvière. Papa and I found him at the hotel," for the poor mother had already guessed that this was her sister's son.

She could not help it. Her greeting was so stiff, her grasp so timid and fluttering, her words so guarded, that M. Rémy, who was used to be cordially welcomed, and much made of, was surprised and disappointed, though he said nothing to show it. His manner froze, his mustaches seemed to curl more stiffly. He had expected to like his aunt from her letters, and from what he had seen of her daughter, and she was just the same as anybody else after all. In the mean time Rémy was introducing himself. He had come to make acquaintance with his English relations, he told Mrs. Maynard. His mother " sent her love, and would they be kind to him?" Marthe, for all her presentiments, could not but relent towards the handsome young fellow; she did not, however, ask him to stay, but this precaution was needless, for her husband had done so already. " We heard him asking for us at the inn," explained Patty. " Mamma, was not it fortunate? Papa was talking about the old brown mare, and I was just walking with Don in the court-yard, and then I heard my cousin saying, 'Where is Sunnymede?' and I said, 'Oh, how delightful!'"

" Hush, darling," said her mother. " Go and tell them to bring us some tea on the lawn."

There was a shady corner not too far from the geraniums, where the table was set, and Rémy liked his aunt a little better, as she attended to his wants, making a gentle clatter among the white cups, and serving out cream strawberries with liberal hand, unlike anything he was used to at home. Mr. Maynard came in, hot, grizzled, and tired, and sank into a garden-chair; his wife's face brightened as he nodded to her; the distant river was flashing and dazzling. Rémy, with his long nose and bright eyes, sat watching the little home-scene, and envying them somewhat the harmony and plenty. There was love in his home, it is true, and food too, but niggardly dealt out and only produced on occasions. If this was English life, Rémy thought it was very pleasant; and as he thought so, he saw the bright and splendid little figure of his cousin Patty advancing radiant across the lawn. For once Mrs. Maynard was almost angry with her daughter for looking so lovely; her shrill sweet voice clamored for attention; her bright head went bobbing over the cake and the strawberries; her bright cheeks were glowing; her eyes seemed to dance, shine, speak, go to sleep, and wake again with a flash. Mrs. Maynard had tied a bright ribbon in her daughter's hair that morning. She wore a white dress like her mother, but all fancifully and prettily cut. As he looked at her, the young man thought at first — unworthy simile — of coffee and cream and strawberries, in a dazzle of sunlight; then he thought of a gipsy, and then of a nymph, shining, transfigured; a wood-nymph escaped from her tree in the forest, for a time consorting with mortals, and eating and joining in their sports, before she fled back to the ivy-grown trunk, which was her home, perhaps.

Mrs. Maynard, frowning slightly, had asked for the second time whether he had seen his grandmother lately, before Rémy, with some little confusion, came back to his senses again. "No, not very lately; not for some time," said he. While Patty cried out, "I want a nice large piece of cake, mamma; this is such a good cake. Have you given Rémy some?"

"Rémy!" her mother looked it rather than said it.

"Yes, dear," said Patty, nothing abashed. "You always called papa Henry, I know, and he wasn't really your cousin. We want to go out on the river in a boat after dinner, please, dearest mamma; and we will get some lilies, and feed the swans. A little more cream, please mamma, and some sugar."

Rémy had not lived all these years in the narrow home school in which he had been bred without learning something of the lesson which was taught there. Taught in the whole manner and being of the household, of its incomings and outgoings, of its interests and selfish preoccupations. We are all sensible, coming from outside into strange homes, of the different spirit or lares penates pervading each household. As surely as every tree in the forest has its sylph, so

every house in the city must own its domestic deity, — different in aspect and character, but ruling with irresistible decision, — orderly and decorous, disorderly; patient, impatient; some stint and mean in contrivances and economies, others profuse and neglectful; others, again, poor, plain of necessity, but kindly and liberal. Some spirits keep the doors of their homes wide open, others ajar, others under lock and key, bolted, barred, with a little cautious peephole to reconnoitre from. As a rule, the very wide open door often invites you to an indifferent entertainment going on within; and people who are particular generally prefer those houses where the door is left, let us say, on the latch.

The household god that Rémy had been brought up to worship was a mean, self-seeking, cautious, and economical spirit. Madame de la Louvière's object and ambition in life had been to bring her servants down to the well-known straw a day; to persuade her husband (no difficult matter) to grasp at every chance and shadow of advantage along his path; to educate her son to believe in the creed which she professed. Rémy must make a good marriage; must keep up with desirable acquaintances; must not neglect his well-to-do uncle, the La Louvière in Burgundy; must occasionally visit his grandmother, Madame Capuchon, whose savings ought to be something considerable by this time. Madame de la Louvière had no idea how considerable these savings were until one day about a week before Rémy made his appearance at Littleton, when the family lawyer, Monsieur Micotton, had come over to see her on business. This grasping, clear-headed woman exercised a strange authority and fascination over the stupid little attorney; he did her business cheaper than for any other client; he told her all sorts of secrets he had no right to communicate; and now he let out to her that her mother had been making her will, and had left everything that she had laid by, in trust for little Marthe Maynard, her elder daughter's only child.

Madame de la Louvière's face pinched and wrinkled up into a sort of struggling knot of horror, severity, and indignation.

"My good Monsieur Micotton, what news you give me! What a culpable partiality! What an injustice; what a horror! Ah, that little intriguing English girl! Did you not remonstrate with, implore, my unfortunate mother? But it must not be allowed. We must interfere."

"Madame," said Micotton, respectfully, "your mother is, as you well know, a person of singular decision and promptness of character. She explained to me that when your sister married, her husband (who apparently is rich) refused to accept more than a portion of the dot which came by right to madame your sister. M. de la Louvière unfortunately at that moment requested some advance, which apparently vexed madame your mother, and — "

"Ah, I understand. It was a plot; it was a conspiracy. I see it all," hissed the angry lady. "Ah, Monsieur Micotton, what a life of anxiety is that of a mother, devoted as I have been; wounded cruelly to the heart; at every hour insulted, trampled on!"

Madame de la Louvière was getting quite wild in her retrospect; and M. Micotton, fearing a nervous attack, hastily gathered his papers together, stuffed them into his shabby bag, and making a great many little parting bows, that were intended to soothe and calm down his angry client, retreated towards the door. As he left he ran up against a tall, broad-shouldered, good-looking young man, with a long nose, quick, dark eyes, and a close-cropped dark beard, thick and soft and bright. Rémy had a look of his mother, who was a tall, straight, well-built woman; but his forehead was broader, his face softer, and his smile was charming. It was like the smile of his unknown aunt, far away in England, the enemy who had, according to his mother's account, cruelly defrauded and robbed him of his rights.

"My son, my poor child!" said the baroness, excitedly; "be calm, come and help me to unravel this plot."

"What is the matter?" Rémy asked, in a cheerful voice. He, however, shrugged his shoulders rather dolefully when he heard the news, for to tell the truth he was in debt, and had been counting upon his grandmother's legacy to help him out. "Hadn't we better make sure of her intentions before we remonstrate?" he suggested, and the baron was accordingly sent for and desired to copy out another of those long letters of his wife's devising, which he signed with a flourish at the end.

Madame Capuchon appealed to, refused to give any information as to the final disposition of her property. She should leave it to anybody she liked. She thought, considering her state of health, that the baron might have waited in patience until she was gone to satisfy his curiosity. She sent her

love to her grandson, but was much displeased with both his parents.

This was a terrible climax. Madame de la Louvière lay awake all one night. Next morning she sent for Rémy and unfolded her plans to him.

"You must go over to England and marry your cousin," she said, decisively; "that is the only thing to be done."

When Micotton came next day for further orders, Madame de la Louvière told him that Rémy was already gone.

All his life long Rémy remembered this evening upon the river, — sweeter, more balmy and wonderful than almost any evening he had ever spent in his life before. He had come with a set purpose, this wolf in sheep's clothing, to perform his part in a bargain, without thought of anything but his own advantage. The idea of any objection being made never occurred to him. He was used to be made much of, as I have said; he could please where he chose. This project accorded so entirely with his French ideas, and seemed so natural and simple an arrangement, that he never thought of doubting its success. For the first time now a possibility occurred to him of something higher, wiser, holier, than money getting and grasping, in his schemes for the future and for his married life. He scarcely owned it to himself, but now that he had seen his cousin, he unconsciously realized that if he had not already come with the set purpose of marrying her, he should undoubtedly have lost his heart to this winsome and brilliant little creature. All that evening, as they slid through the water, paddling between the twilight fields, pushing through the beds of water-lilies, sometimes spurting swiftly through the rustling reeds, with the gorgeous banks on either side, and the sunset beyond the hills, and the figures strolling tranquilly along the meadows, De la Louvière only felt himself drifting and drifting into a new and wonderful world. This time-wise young fellow felt as if he was being washed white and happy and peaceful in the lovely purple river. Everything was at once twilit, moonlit, and sunlit. The water flowed deep and clear. Patty, with a bulrush wand, sat at the stern, bending forward and talking happily; the people on the shore heard her sweet chatter.

Once Patty uttered a cry of alarm. "Don! Where was Don?" He had been very contentedly following them, trotting along the bank; but now in the twilight they could not make him out. Patty called and her father halloed, and Rémy pulled out a little silver whistle he happened to have in his pocket, and whistled shrilly. Old Don, who had been a little ahead, hearing all this hullabaloo, quietly plashed from the banks into the water, and came swimming up to the side of the boat, with his honest old nose in the air and his ears floating on the little ripples. Having satisfied them of his safety and tried to wag his tail in the water, he swam back to shore again, and the boat sped on its way home through the twilight.

"What a nice little whistle!" said Patty.

"Do take it," said Rémy. "It is what I call my dogs at home with. Please take it. It will give me pleasure to think that anything of mine is used by you."

"Oh, thank you," said Patty, as she put out her soft, warm hand through the cool twilight and took it from him. Maynard was looking out for the lock and paying no attention. Rémy felt as glad as if some great good fortune had happened to him.

The light was burning in the drawing-room when they got back. Mrs. Maynard had ordered some coffee to be ready for them, and was waiting with a somewhat anxious face for their return.

"O mamma, it has been so heavenly," said Patty, once more sinking into her own corner by the window.

And then the moon came brightly hanging in the sky, and a nightingale began to sing. Rémy had never been so happy in his life before. He had forgotten all about his speculation, and was only thinking that his English cousin was more charming than all his grandmother's money-bags piled in a heap. For that night he forgot his part of wolf altogether.

In the morning, Patty took her cousin to the greenhouse, to the stable to see her pony; she did the honors of Sunnymede with so much gayety and frankness that her mother had not the heart to put conscious thoughts into the child's head, and let her go her own way. The two came back late to the early dinner; Mr. Maynard frowned, he disliked unpunctuality. Rémy was too happy to see darkness anywhere, or frowns in anybody's face, but then his eyes were dazzled. It was too good to last, he thought, and in truth a storm was rising even then.

During dinner, the post came in. Mrs. Maynard glanced at her correspondence, and then at her husband, as she put it into her pocket. "It is from my mother," she said. Rémy looked a little interested, but asked no questions, and went on talking and laughing with his cousin; and after dinner, when Mrs. Maynard took her letter away to read in the study, the two young people went and sat upon the little terrace in front of the house.

The letter was from Madame Capuchon, and Mrs. Maynard having read it, put it into her husband's hands with a little exclamation of bewildered dismay.

"What is the matter, my dear?" said Maynard, looking up from his paper which had come by the same afternoon post.

"Only read this," she said; "you will know best what to do. O Henry, he must go; he should never have come."

My heroine's mother was never very remarkable for spirit; her nearest approach to it was this first obstinate adherence to anything which Henry might decree. Like other weak people she knew that if she once changed her mind she was lost, and accordingly she clung to it in the smallest decisions of life with an imploring persistence; poor Marthe, her decision was a straw in a great sea of unknown possibilities. Madame Capuchon was a strong-minded woman, and not afraid to change her mind.

"I have heard from Félicie," the old lady wrote; "but she says nothing of a certain fine scheme which I hasten to acquaint you with. I learned it by chance the other day, when Micotton was with me consulting on the subject of my will, which it seems has given great offence to the De la Louvières. Considering the precarious state of my health, they might surely have taken patience; but I am now determined that they shall not benefit by one farthing that I possess. Micotton, at my desire, confessed that Rémy has gone over to England for the express purpose of making advances to Marthe, your daughter, in hopes of eventually benefiting through me. He is a young man of indifferent character, and he inherits, no doubt, the covetous and grasping spirit of his father." Mr. Maynard read no farther; he flushed up, and began to hiss out certain harmless oaths between his teeth. "Does that confounded young puppy think my Patty is to be disposed of like a bundle of hay? Does he come here scheming after that poor old woman's money? Be hanged to the fellow! he must be told to go about his business, Marthe, or the child may be taking a fancy to him. Confound the impertinent jackanapes!"

"But who is to tell him?" poor Marthe faltered, with one more dismal presentiment.

"You, to be sure," said Maynard, clapping on his felt hat, and marching right away off the premises.

In the mean time Rémy and his cousin had been very busy making Don jump backwards and forwards over the low parapet. They had a little disjointed conversation between the jumping.

"What is your home like?" Patty asked once.

"I wish it was more like yours," said Rémy, with some expression; "it would make me very happy to think that, some day, it might become more so."

The girl seemed almost to understand his meaning, for she blushed and laughed, and tossed her gloves up in the air, and caught them again. "I love my home dearly," said she.

At that moment the garden-door opened, and Mr. Maynard appeared, but instead of coming towards them, he no sooner saw the two young folks than he began walking straight away in the direction of the outer gate, never turning his head or paying any attention to the young folks.

"Papa, papa!" cried Patty, springing up; but her father walked on, never heeding, and yet she was sure he must have heard. What could it mean? She looked at Rémy, who was quite unconscious, twirling his mustache, and stirring up Don with the toe of his boot; from Rémy she looked round to the library window, which was open wide, and where her mother was standing.

"Do you want me?" Patty cried, running up.

"Ask your cousin to come and speak to me," said Mrs. Maynard, very gravely, — "here, in papa's room."

Patty was certain that something was wrong. She gave Rémy her mother's message, with a wistful glance to see whether he did not suspect any trouble. The young man started up obediently, and Patty waited outside in the sun, listening to the voices droning away within, watching the sparkle of the distant river, lazily following the flight of a big bumble-bee, — wondering when their talk would be over and Rémy would come out to her again. From where she sat Patty could see the reflection of the two talkers in the big sloping looking-glass

over the library-table. Her mother was standing very dignified and stately; the young man had drawn himself straight up — so straight, so grim and fierce-looking, that Patty, as she looked, was surer and more sure that all was not right; and she saw her mother give him a letter, and he seemed to push it away. And then it was not Rémy, but Mrs. Maynard who came out, looking very pale, and who said, "Patty, darling, I have been very much pained. Your cousin has behaved so strangely and unkindly to you and me, and to your father, that we can never forget or forgive it. Your father says so."

Mrs. Maynard had tried to perform her task as gently as she could. She told Rémy that English people had different views on many subjects from the French; that she had learned his intentions from her mother, and thought it best to tell him plainly at once that she and Mr. Maynard could never consent to any such arrangement; and under the circumstances — that — that — that —

"You can never consent," repeated the young man, stepping forward, and looking through her and round about her, seeing all her doubts, all her presentiments, reading the letter, overhearing her conversation with her husband all in one instant, — so it seemed to poor Marthe. "And why not, pray?"

"We cannot argue the question," his aunt said, with some dignity. "You must not attempt to see my daughter any more."

"You mean to say that you are turning me, your sister's son, out of your house," the indignant Rémy said. "I own to all that you accuse me of. I hoped to marry your daughter. I still hope it; and I shall do so still," cried the young man.

Rémy's real genuine admiration for Patty stood him in little stead; he was angry and lost his temper in his great disappointment and surprise. He behaved badly and foolishly.

"I had not meant to turn you out of my house," said his aunt, gravely; "but for the present I think you had certainly better go. I cannot expose my daughter to any agitation."

"You have said more than enough," said Rémy. "I am going this instant." And as he spoke he went striding out of the room.

And so Rémy came back no more to sit with Patty under the ash-tree; but her mother, with her grave face, stood before her, and began telling her this impossible, unbelievable fact, — that he was young, that he had been to blame.

-" He unkind! he to blame! O mamma," the girl said, in a voice of reproach.

" He has been unkind and scheming, and he was rude to me, darling. I am sorry, but it is a fact." And Marthe, as she spoke, glanced a little anxiously at Patty, who had changed color, and then at De la Louvière himself,who was marching up,fierce still, and pale, with bristling hair, — his nose looking hooked, and his lips parting in a sort of scornful way. He was carrying his cloak on his arm.

"I have come to wish you good-by, and to thank you for your English hospitality, madame," said he, with a grand, sweeping bow. "My cousin, have you not got a word for me?"

But Mrs. Maynard's eyes were upon her, and Patty, with a sudden shy stiffness for which she hated herself then, and for many and many a day and night after, said good-by, looking down with a sinking heart, and Rémy marched away with rage and scorn in his. "They are all alike; not one bit better than myself. That little girl has neither kindness, nor feeling, nor fidelity in her. The money: they want to keep it for them-selves, — that is the meaning of all these fine speeches. I should like to get hold of her all the same, little stony-hearted flirt,just to spite them; yes, and throw her over at the last moment, money and all, — impertinent, ill-bred folks!" And it happened that just at this minute Mr. Maynard was coming back thoughtfully the way he had gone, and the two men stopped face to face, one red, the other pale. Mrs Maynard, seeing the meet-ing, came hastily up.

"You will be glad to hear that I am go-ing," said Rémy, defiantly looking at his uncle as he had done at his aunt.

"I am very glad to hear it," said Mr. Maynard. "I have no words to express the indignation which fills me at the thought of your making a speculation of my daugh-ter's affections, and the sooner you are gone the better."

"Hush, dear," said Mrs. Maynard, laying her hand on her husband's arm, and looking at Patty, who had followed her at a little distance. She had had her own say, and was beginning to think poor Rémy hardly dealt with.

"Let him say what he likes, madame; I don't care," De la Louvière said. "I am certainly going. You have failed, both of you, in kindness and hospitality; as for my cousin—;" but looking at Patty, he saw that her eyes were full of tears, and he

stopped short. "I am all that you think," Rémy went on. "I am in debt, I have lost money at gambling, I am a good-for-nothing fellow. You might have made something of me, all of you; but you are a sordid na-tion and don't understand the feelings of a French gentleman."

With this bravado Rémy finally stalked off.

"I think, perhaps, we were a little hasty," said the injudicious Marthe, while Patty suddenly burst out crying and ran away.

Poor little Patty came down to tea that evening looking very pale, with pouting red lips, prettier than ever, her mother thought, as she silently gave the child her cupful of tea, and cut her bread-and-butter, and put liberal helpings of jam and fruit before her, dainties that were served in the old cut-glass dishes that had sparkled on Maynard's grandmother's tea-table before. The old Queen Anne teapot, too, was an heirloom, and the urn and the pretty straight spoons, and the hideous old china tea-set with the red and yellow flowers. There were other heirlooms in the family; and even Patty's bright eyes had been her great-grandmoth-er's a century ago, as anybody might see who looked at the picture on the wall. Mr. Maynard was silent; he had been angry with his wife for her gentle remonstrance, furious with the young man for the high hand in which he had carried matters, dis-pleased with Patty for crying, and with himself for not having foreseen the turn things were taking; and he now sat sulkily stirring his tea — sulky but relenting — and not indisposed for peace. After all, he had had his own way, and that is a wonderful calming process. Rémy was gone; nothing left of him but a silver whistle that Patty had put away in her work-table drawer. He was gone; the echo of his last angry words were dinning in Maynard's ears, while a psalm of relief was sounding in the mother's heart. Patty sulked like her father, and ate her bread-and-jam without speaking a word. There was no great harm done, Mrs. Maynard thought, as she kept her daughter supplied. She herself had been so disturbed and overcome by the stormy events of the day that she could not eat. She made the mistake that many elders have made before her; they mistake physical for mental disturbance; poor well-hacked bodies that have been jolted, shaken, patched, and mended, and strained in half-a-dozen places, are easily affected by the passing jars of the moment; they suffer and lose their appetite, and get aches directly, which take away much sense of the mental inquietude which brought the disturbance about. Young healthy creatures like Patty can eat a good dinner and feel a keen pang and hide it, and chatter on scarcely conscious of their own heroism. But as the days went by Mrs. Maynard suspected that all was not well with the child; there seemed to be a little effort and strain in the life which had seemed so easy and smooth before. More than once, Mrs. Maynard noticed her daughter's eyes fixed upon her curiously and wistfully. One day the mother asked her why she looked at her so. Patty blushed but did not answer. The truth was, it was the likeness to her cousin which she was studying. These blushes and silence made Marthe Maynard a little uneasy.

But more days passed, and the mother's anxious heart was relieved. Patty had brightened up again, and looked like herself, coming and going in her Undine-like way, bringing home long wreaths of ivy, birds' eggs, sylvan treasures. She was out in all weathers. Her locks only curled the crisper for the falling rain, and her cheeks only brightened when the damp rose up from the river. The time came for their annual visit to Madame de Capuchon. Patty, out in her woods and meadows, wondered and wondered what might come of it. But Poictiers is a long way from Fontainebleau, "fortunately," "alas!" thought the mother, — in her room, packing Patty's treasures, — and the daughter out in the open field in the same breath. They were so used to one another, these two, that some sort of magnetic current passed between them at times, and certainly Marthe never thought of Rémy de la Louvière that Patty did not think of him too.

III.

OLD Madame de Capuchon was delighted with her grand-daughter, and the improvement she found in her since the year before. She made more of her than she had ever done of Marthe her daughter. All manner of relics were produced out of the old lady's ancient stores to adorn Miss Patty's crisp locks, and little round white throat and wrists; small medallions were hung round her neck, brooches and laces pinned on, ribbons tied and muslins measured, while

Simonne tried her hand once again at cake-making. Patty, in return, brought a great rush of youth, and liberty, and sunshine, into the old closed house, where she was spoilt, worshipped, petted, to her heart's content. Her mother's tender, speechless love seemed dimmed and put out by this chorus of compliments and admiration. "Take care of your complexion; whatever you do; take care of your complexion," her grandmother was always saying. Madame Capuchon actually sent for the first modiste in the town, explained what she wanted, and ordered a scarlet "capeline," — such as ladies wear by the sea-side, — a pretty frilled, quilted, laced, and braided scarlet hood, close round the cheeks, and tied up to the chin, to protect her grand-daughter's youthful bloom from the scorching rays of the sun. She need not have been so anxious. Patty's roses were of a damask that does not fade in the sun's rays.

'Squire Maynard, who was a sensible man, did not approve of all this to do, and thought it was all very bad for Miss Patty, "whose little head was quite full enough of nonsense already," he said. One day Patty came home with the celebrated pearls around her neck, that Madame de la Louvière had tried so hard to get. Madame Capuchon forgot that she had already given them to Marthe, but Mrs. Maynard herself was the last to have remembered this, and it was her husband who said to her, with a shrug of the shoulders, —

"It is all very well; but they are yours, my dear, and your mother has no more right to them than Patty has."

Patty pouted, flashed, tossed her little head, flung her arms round her mother's neck, all in an instant. She was a tender-hearted little person, heedless, impulsive, both for the best and the worst, as her poor mother knew to her cost. The 'squire thought his wife spoilt her daughter, s· occasionally tried a course of judicious verity, and, as I have already said, he only succeeded in frightening the child m than he had any idea of.

"Take them, dear mamma," said Patty, pulling off her necklace. "I didn't know anything about them. Grandmamma tied them on."

"Darling," said her mother, "you are my jewel. I don't want these pearls; and if they are mine, I give them to you."

Two pearl drops were in Mrs. Maynard's eyes as she spoke. She was thinking of her long lonely days, and of the treasures which were now hers. Looking at this bright face in its scarlet hood, — this gay, youthful presence standing before them all undimmed, in the splendor of its confidence and brightness, — it seemed to Mrs. Maynard as if now, in her old age, now that she had even forgotten her longings for them, all the good things were granted to her, the want of which had made her early life so sad. It was like a miracle, that at fifty all this should come to her. Her meek, glad eyes sought her husband's. He was frowning, and eying his little girl uneasily.

"I don't like that red bonnet of yours," said he. "It is too conspicuous. You can't walk about Paris in that."

"Paris!" shrieked Patty. "Am I going to Paris, papa?"

"You must take great care of your father, Patty," said her mother. "I shall stay here with my mother until you come back."

I am not going to describe Patty's delight and surprise. Everybody has seen through her eyes, at one time or another, and knows what it is to be sixteen, and transported into a dazzling, ringing world of sounds, and sights, and tastes, and revelations. The good father took his daughter to dine off delicious little dishes with sauces, with white bread and butter to eat in between the courses; he hired little carriages, in which they sped through the blazing streets, and were set down at the doors of museums and palaces, and the gates of cool gardens, where fountains murmured and music played; he had some friends in Paris — a good-natured old couple — who volunteered to take charge of his girl; but for that whole, happy, unspeakable week he rarely left her. One night he took her to the play, — a grand fairy piece, — where a fustian peasant maiden was turned into a satin princess in a flash of music and electric light. Patty took her father's arm, and came away with the crowd, with the vision of those waving halos of bliss opening and shining with golden rain and silver-garbed nymphs, and shrieks of music and admiration, all singing and turning before her. The satin princess was already re-transformed, but that was no affair of Patty's. Some one in the crowd, better used to plays and fairy pieces, coming along behind the father and daughter, thought that by far the prettiest sight he had seen that night was this lovely, eager little face before him, and that those two dark eyes — now flashing, now silent — were the most beautiful illuminations he had witnessed for many a day.

The bright eyes never discovered who it was behind her. Need I say that it was Rémy, who, after looking for them for a couple of days in all the most likely places, took a ticket for Fontainebleau on the third evening after he had seen them. What fascination was it that attracted him? He was hurt and angry with her, he loved and he longed to see her. Sometimes vague thoughts of revenge crossed his mind; he would see her and win her affections, and then turn away and leave her, and pay back the affront which had been put upon him. M. Rémy, curling his mustaches in the railway-carriage, and meditating this admirable scheme, was no very pleasant object to contemplate.

"That gentleman in the corner looks ready to eat us all up," whispered a little bride to her husband.

Meanwhile Patty had been going on her way very placidly all these three days, running hither and thither, driving in the forest, dining with her grandmother, coming home at night under the stars. The little red hood was well known in the place. Sometimes escorted by Betty, an English maid who had come over with the family; oftener Mr. Maynard himself walked with his daughter. Fontainebleau was not Littleton, and he did not like her going about alone, although Patty used to pout and rebel at these precautions. Mrs. Maynard herself rarely walked; she used to drive over to her mother's of an afternoon, and her husband and daughter would follow her later; and Simonne, radiant, would then superintend the preparation of fricandeaus and galettes, such as she loved to set before them, and cream tarts and chicken and *vol au vent.* There was no end to her resources. And yet to hear Madame Capuchon, one would think that she led the life of an invalid ascetic starving on a desert island. "These railways carry away everything," the old lady would say; "they leave one nothing. When I say that I have dined, it is for the sake of saying so. You know I am not particular, but they leave us nothing, absolutely nothing, to eat." On this especial occasion the old lady was in a state of pathetic indignation over M. Bougu, her butterman, who had been taken up for false practices. Simonne joined in: "I went in for the tray," she said. "Oh, I saw at once, by the expression of madame's face, that there was something wrong. It was lard that he had mixed with his butter. As it is, I do not know where to go to find her anything fit to eat. They keep cows at the hotel," she added, turning to Marthe as she set down a great dish full of cream-cakes upon the table. "Perhaps they would supply us, if you asked them."

Mrs. Maynard undertook the negotiation; and the next day she called Patty to her into the little drawing-room, and gave the child a piece of honeycomb and a little pat in a vine-leaf, to take to Madame Capuchon, as a sample. "Give her my love and tell her she can have as much more as she likes; and call Betty to go with you," said Mrs. Maynard. "Tell Betty to follow me," said Patty, dancing off delighted with her commission. Betty followed; but there are two roads to Madame Capuchon's, one by the street and one by the park. Patty certainly waited for three minutes, but Betty never came; she was trudging down the town, and gaping into all the shops as she went along, while her young mistress had escaped into the park, and was hurrying along the avenues, delighted to be free, — hurrying and then stopping, as the fancy took her. The sun shone, the golden water quivered, the swans came sailing by. It was all Patty could do not to sing right out and dance to her own singing. By degrees her spirits quieted down a little.

Patty was standing leaning over the stone parapet at the end of the terrace, and looking down into the water which laps against it. A shoal of carp was passing through the clear, cool depths. Solemn patriarchs, bald, dim with age, bleared and faded and overgrown with strange mosses and lichens, terrible with their chill life of centuries, solemnly sliding, followed by their court through the clear, cool waters where they had floated for ages past; unconscious, living, indifferent while the generations were succeeding one another, and angry multitudes surging and yelling while kingdoms changed hands; while the gay court ladies, scattering crumbs with their dainty fingers, were hooted by the hags and furies of the Revolution, shrieking for bread and for blood for their children; the carp may have dived for safety into the cool depths of the basins while these awful ghosts of want and madness clamored round the doors of the palace, — ghosts that have not passed away forever, alas! with the powders and patches, and the stately well-bred follies of the court of Dives. After these times a new order of things was established, and the carps may have seen a new race of spirits in the quaint

garb and odd affectation of a by-gone age, of senates and consuls and a dead Roman people; and then an Emperor, broken-hearted, signed away an empire, and a Waterloo was fought; and to-day began to dawn, and the sun shone for a while upon the kingly dignity of Orleans; and then upon a second empire, with flags and many eagles and bees to decorate the whole, and trumpets blowing and looms at work and a temple raised to the new goddess of industry.

What did it all matter to the old gray carp? They had been fed by kings and by emperors; and now they were snatching as eagerly at the crumbs which Patty Maynard was dropping one by one into the water, and which floated pleasantly into their great open maws. The little bits of bread tasted much alike from wherever they came. If Patty had been used to put such vague speculations into words, she might have wondered sometimes whether we human carp, snatching at the crumbs which fall upon the waters of life, are not also greedy and unconscious of the wonders and changes that may be going on close at hand in another element to which we do not belong, but at which we guess now and then.

A crumb fell to little Patty herself, just then gazing down deep into the water. The sun began to shine hot and yet more hot, and the child put up her big white umbrella, for her hood did not shade her eyes. A great magnificent stream of light illumined the grand old place, and the waving tree-tops, and the still currentless lake. The fish floated on basking, the birds in the trees seemed suddenly silenced by the intense beautiful radiance; the old palace courts gleamed bravely, the shadows shrank and blackened; hot, sweet, and silent the light streamed upon the great green arches and courts and colonnades of the palace of garden without, upon the arches and courts and colonnades of the palace of marble within, with its quaint eaves and mullions, its lilies of France and D's and H's still entwined, though D and H had been parted for three centuries and more. It was so sweet and so serene, that Patty began to think of her cousin. She could not have told you why five days put her in mind of him, and of that happy hour in the boat; and to-day she could not help it, she pulled the little silver whistle out of her pocket, and instead of pushing the thought of Rémy away, as she had done valiantly of late, the silly child turned the whistle in her hands round and round again. It gleamed in the sun like a whistle of fire; and then slowly she put it to her lips. Should she frighten the carp? Patty wondered; and as she blew a very sweet long note upon the shrill gleaming toy, it echoed oddly in the stillness, and across the water. The carp did not seem to hear it; but Patty stopped short, frightened, ashamed, with burning blushes, for, looking up at the sound of a footstep striking across the stone terrace, she saw her cousin coming towards her.

To people who are in love each meeting is a new miracle. This was an odd chance certainly, a quaint freak of fortune. The child thought it was some incantation that she had unconsciously performed. She sprang back, her dark eyes flashed, the silver whistle fell to the ground and went rolling and rolling, and bobbing across the stones to the young man's feet.

He picked it up and came forward with an amused and lover-like smile, holding it out in his hand. "I have only just heard you were here," he said; "I came to see my grandmother, last night, from Paris. My dear cousin, what a delightful chance. Are not you a little bit glad to see me?" said the young man, romantically. It was a shame to play off his airs and graces upon such a simple, downright soul as Marthe Maynard. Some one should have boxed his ears as he stood there smiling, handsome, irresistible, trying to make a sentimental scene out of a chance meeting. Poor little Patty, with all her courage and simpleness, was no match for him at first; she looked up at his face wistfully and then turned away, for one burning blush succeeded to another, and then she took courage again. "Of course I am glad to see you, cousin Rémy," said she, brightly, and she held out her little brown hand and put it frankly into his. "It is the greatest pleasure and delight to me, above all now when I had given up all hopes forever; but it's no use," said Patty, with a sigh, "for I know I mustn't talk to you; they wouldn't like it. I must never whistle again upon the little whistle, for fear you should appear," she said, with a sigh.

This was no cold-hearted maiden. Rémy forgot his vague schemes of revenge and desertion the moment he heard the sound of her dear little voice. "They wouldn't like it," said Rémy, reddening, "and I have been longing and wearying to see you again Patty. What do you suppose I have come here for?—Patty, Patty, confess that you were thinking of me when you whistled;" and as he said this the wolf's whole heart melted. "Do you know how often I have thought of you since I was cruelly driven away from your house?"

Two great, ashamed, vexed, sorrowful tears started into Marthe's eyes as she turned away her head and pulled away her hand.

"O Rémy; indeed, indeed there must have been some reason, some mistake. Dear papa, if you knew how he loves me and mamma, and, oh, how miserable it made me!"

"I dare say there was some mistake, since you say so," said the wily wolf. "Patty, only say you love me a little, and I will forgive everything and anything."

"I mustn't let any one talk about forgiving *them*," said the girl. "I would love you a great deal if I might," she added, with another sigh. "I do love you, only I try not to, and I think,—I am sure I shall get over it in time, if I can only be brave."

This was such an astounding confession that De la Louvière hardly knew how to take it; touched and amused and amazed, he stood there, looking at the honest little sweet face. Patty's confession was a very honest one. The girl knew that it was not to be; she was loyal to her father, and, above all, to that tender, wistful mother. Filial devotion seemed like the bright eyes and silver teapot to be an inheritance in her family. She did not deceive herself; she knew that she loved her cousin with something more than cousinly affection, but she also believed that it was a fancy which could be conquered. "We are human beings," said Patty, like St. Paul; "we are not machines; we can do what we will with ourselves, if we only determine to try. And I will try." And she set her teeth and looked quite fierce at Rémy; and then she melted again, and said, in her childish way, "You never told me you would come if I blew upon the whistle."

Do her harm,—wound her,—punish her parents by stabbing this tender little heart? Rémy said to himself that he had rather cut off his mustache.

There was something loyal, honest, and tender in the little thing, that touched him inexpressibly. He suddenly began to tell himself that he agreed with his uncle that to try to marry Patty for money's sake had been a shame and a sin. He had been a fool and a madman, and blind and deaf. Rémy de la Louvière was only half a wolf after all,

—a sheep in wolf's clothing. He had worn the skin so long that he had begun to think it was his very own, and he was perfectly amazed and surprised to find such a soft, tender place beneath it.

It was with quite a different look and tone from the romantic, impassioned, corsair manner in which he had begun, that he said, very gently, "Dear Patty, don't try too hard not to like me. I cannot help hoping that all will be well. You will hope too, will you not?"

"Yes, indeed I will," said Patty; "and now, Rémy, you must go. I have talked to you long enough. See, this is the back gate and the way to the Rue de la Lampe;" for they had been walking on all this time and following the course of the avenue. One or two people passing by looked kindly at the handsome young couple strolling in the sunshine; a man in a blouse, wheeling a hand-truck, looked over his shoulder a second time as he turned down the turning to the Rue de la Lampe. Patty did not see him; she was absorbed in one great resolution. She must go now, and say good-by to her cousin.

"Come a little way farther with me," said Rémy; "just a little way under the trees. Patty, I have a confession to make to you. You will hate me, perhaps, and yet I cannot help telling you."

"Oh, indeed, I must not come now," Patty said. "Good-by, good-by."

"You won't listen to me, then?" said the young man; so sadly, that she had not the courage to leave him, and she turned at last, and walked a few steps.

"Will you let me carry your basket?" said her cousin. "Who are you taking this to?"

"It is for my grandmother," said the girl, resisting. "Rémy, have you really anything to say?"

They had come to the end of the park, where its gates lead into the forest; one road led to the Rue de la Lampe, the other into the great waving world of trees. It was a lovely summer's afternoon. There was a host in the air, delighting and basking in the golden comfort; butterflies, midges, flights of birds from the forest were passing. It was pleasant to exist in such a place and hour, to walk by Rémy on the soft springing turf, and to listen to the sound of his voice under the shade of the overarching boughs.

"Patty, do you know I did want to marry you for your money?" Rémy said at last.

"I love you truly; but I have not loved you always as I ought to have done,—as I do now. You scorn me; you cannot forgive me?" he added, as the girl stopped short. "You will never trust me again."

"O Rémy! how could you. . . . Oh, yes, indeed, indeed I do forgive you! I do trust you," she added quickly, saying anything to comfort and cheer him when he looked so unhappy. Every moment took them farther and farther on. The little person with the pretty red hood and bright eyes and the little basket had almost forgotten her commission, her conscience, her grandmother, and all the other duties of life. Rémy, too, had forgotten everything but the bright, sweet little face, the red hood, and the little hand holding the basket, when they came to a dark, enclosed halting-place at the end of the avenue, from whence a few rocky steps led out upon a sudden hillside, which looked out into the open world. It was a lovely, surprising sight; a burst of open country, a great purple amphitheatre of rocks shining and hills spreading to meet the skies, clefts, and sudden gleams, and a wide distant horizon of waving forest fringing the valley. Clouds were drifting and tints changing, the heather springing between the rocks at their feet, and the thousands of tree-tops swaying like a ripple on a sea. Something in the great wide freshness of the place brought Patty to herself again.

"How lovely it is!" she said. "O Rémy! why did you let me come? Oh, I oughtn't to have come."

Rémy tried to comfort her. "We have not been very long," he said. "We will take the short cut through the trees, and you shall tell your mother all about it. There's no more reason why we shouldn't walk together now than when we were at Littleton."

As he was speaking he was leading the way through the brushwood, and they got into a cross avenue leading back to the carriage-road.

"I shall come to Madame Capuchon's, too, since you are going," said Rémy, making a grand resolution. "I think perhaps she will help us. She is bound to, since she did all the mischief." And then he went on a few steps, holding back the trees that grew in Patty's way. A little field-mouse peeped at them and ran away, a lightning sheet of light flashed through the green and changing leaves, little blue flowers were twinkling on mosses under the trees, dried blossoms were falling, and cones and dead leaves and aromatic twigs and shoots.

"Is this the way?" said Patty, suddenly stopping short, and looking about her. "Rémy, look at those arrows cut in the trees; they are not pointing to the road we have come. O Rémy! do not lose the way!" cried Patty, in a sudden fright.

"Don't be afraid," Rémy answered, laughing, and hurrying on before her; and then he stopped short, and began to pull at his mustache, looking first in one direction, and then in another. "Do you think they would be anxious if you were a little late?" he said.

"Anxious!" cried Patty. "Mammy would die; she could not bear it. Ó Rémy, Rémy! what shall I do?" She flushed up, and almost began to cry. Oh, find the way, please. Do you see any more arrows? Here is one; come, come."

Patty turned, and began to retrace her steps, hurrying along in a fever of terror and remorse. The wood-pigeons cooed overhead; the long lines of distant trees were mingling and twisting in a sort of dance, as she flew along.

"Wait for me, Patty," cried Rémy. "Here is some one to ask." And as he spoke he pointed to an old woman coming along one of the narrow cross pathways, carrying a tray of sweetmeats and a great jar of lemonade.

"Fontainebleau, my little gentleman?" said the old woman. "You are turning your back upon it. The arrows point away from Fontainebleau, and not towards the town. Do you know the big cross near the gate? Well, it is just at the end of that long avenue. Wait, wait, my little gentleman. Won't you buy a sweet sugarstick for the pretty little lady in the red hood? Believe me, she is fond of sugarsticks. It is not the first time that she has bought some of mine."

But Rémy knew that Patty was in no mood for barley-sugar, and he went off to cheer up his cousin with the good news. The old woman hobbled off grumbling.

It was getting later by this time. The shadows were changing, and a western light was beginning to glow upon the many stems and quivering branches of the great waving forest. Everything glowed in unwearied change and beauty, but they had admired enough. A bird was singing high above over their heads; they walked on quickly in silence for half an hour or more, and at the end of the avenue—as the old

woman had told them—they found a wide, stony ascending road, with the dark murmuring fringe of the woods on either side, and a great cross at the summit of the ascent. Here Patty sank down for a minute, almost falling upon the step, and feeling safe. This gate was close to the Rue de la Lampe.

"Now go," she said to her cousin. "Go on first, and I will follow, dear Rémy. I don't want to be seen with you any more. People know me and my red hood."

De la Louvière could only hope that Patty had not already been recognized.

All the same he refused utterly to leave her until they reached the gates of the forest; then he took the short way to the Rue de la Lampe, and Patty followed slowly. She had had a shock; she wanted to be calm before she saw her grandmother. Her heart was beating still; she was tired and sorry. Patty's conscience was not easy; she felt she had done wrong, and yet, —and yet, —with the world of love in her heart it seemed as if nothing could be wrong and nobody angry or anxious.

Mrs. Maynard herself had felt something of the sort that afternoon after the little girl had left her. The mother watched her across the court-yard, and then sat down as usual to her work. Her eyes filled up with grateful tears as she bent over her sewing; they often did when Henry spoke a kind word or Patty looked specially happy. Yes, it was a miracle that at fifty all this should come to her, thought Marthe Maynard, — brilliant beauty and courage and happiness, and the delight of youth and of early hopes unrepressed. It was like a miracle that all this had come to her in a dearer and happier form than if it had been given to herself. Marthe wondered whether all her share had been reserved for her darling in some mysterious fashion, and so she went on stitching her thoughts to her canvas as people do; peaceful, tranquil, happy thoughts they were, as she sat waiting for her husband's return. An hour or two went by, people came and went in the court-yard below, the little diligence rattled off to the railway; at last, thinking she heard Henry's voice, Marthe leaned out of the window and saw him speaking to an old woman with a basket of sweetmeats, and then she heard the sitting-room door open, and she looked round to see who it was coming in. It was Simonne, who came bustling in with a troubled look, like ripples in a placid smooth pool. The good old creature had put on a shawl and gloves and a clean cap with huge frills, and stood silent, umbrella in hand, and staring at the calm-looking lady at her work-table.

"What is it?" said Marthe, looking up. "Simonne, is my mother unwell?"

"Madame is quite well; do not be uneasy," said Simonne, with a quick, uncertain glance in Mrs. Maynard's face.

"Have you brought me back Patty?" said Mrs. Maynard. "Has Betty come with you?"

"Betty? I don't know where she is," said Simonne. "She is a craze-pated girl, and you should not allow her to take charge of Patty."

Mrs. Maynard smiled. She knew Simonne's ways of old. All cooks, housekeepers, ladies'-maids, etc., under fifty, were crazy-pated girls with Simonne, whose sympathies certainly did not rest among her own class. Mrs. Maynard's smile, however, changed away when she looked at Simonne a second time.

"I am sure something is the matter," Marthe cried, starting up. "Where's Patty?" The poor mother, suddenly conjecturing evil, had turned quite pale, and all the soft contentment and calm were gone in one instant. She seized Simonne's arm with an imploring, nervous clutch, as if praying that it might be nothing dreadful.

"Don't be uneasy, madame," said Simonne. "Girls are girls, and that Betty is too scatterbrained to be trusted another time. She missed Patty, and came alone to our house. Oh, I sent her off quickly enough to meet mademoiselle. But you see, madame," Simonne was hurrying on nervously over her words, "our Patty is so young she thinks of no harm; she runs here and there just as fancy takes her; but a young girl must not be talked of, and — and it does not do for her to be seen alone in company with anybody but her mother or father. There's no harm done, but —"

"What are you talking of? Why do you frighten me for nothing, Simonne?" said Mrs. Maynard, recovering crossly with a faint gasp of relief, and thinking all was well. She had expected a broken limb at the least in her sudden alarm.

"There, Marthe," said Simonne, taking her hand, "you must not be angry with me. It was the concierge de chez nous who made a remark which displeased me, and I thought I had best come straight to you."

"My Patty! my Patty! What have you *been doing,* Simonne? How dare you talk of my child to common people?" said the anxious mother.

"I was anxious, madame," said poor Simonne, humbly. "I looked for her up the street and along the great avenue, and our concierge met me and said, 'Don't trouble yourself. I met your young lady going towards the forest in company with a young man.' She is a naughty child, and I was vexed, madame, that is all," said Simonne.

But Mrs. Maynard hardly heard her to the end; she put up her two hands with a little cry of anxious horror. "And is she not back? What have you been doing? Why did you not come before? My Patty! my Patty! what absurd mistake is this? Oh, where is my husband? Papa, papa!" cried poor Mrs. Maynard, distracted, running out upon the landing. Mr. Maynard was coming upstairs at that instant, followed by the blowsy and breathless Betty.

Mr. Maynard had evidently heard the whole story; he looked black and white, as people do who are terribly disturbed and annoyed. Had they been at home in England, Patty's disappearance would have seemed nothing to them; there were half a dozen young cousins and neighbors to whose care she might have been trusted; but here, where they knew no one, it was inexplicable, and no wonder they were disquieted and shocked. Mr. Maynard tried to reassure his wife, and vented his anxiety in wrath upon the luckless Betty.

Marthe sickened as she listened to Betty's sobs and excuses. "I can't help it," said the stupid girl, with a scared face. "Miss Patty didn't wait for me. The old woman says she saw a red hood in the forest, going along with a young man; master heard her."

"Hold your tongue, you fool! How dare you all come to me with such lies!" shouted Maynard. He hated the sight of the girl ever after, and he rushed down into the court again. The old woman was gone, but a carriage was standing there waiting to be engaged.

"We may as well go and fetch Patty at your mother's," Maynard called out with some appearance of calmness. "I dare say she is there by this time." Mrs. Maynard ran downstairs and got in; Simonne bundled in too, and sat with her back to the horses. But that ten minutes' drive was so horrible that not one of them ever spoke of it again.

They need not have been so miserable, poor people, if they had only known Patty had safely reached her grandmother's door by that time. When the concierge, who was sitting on his barrow at the door, let her in and looked at her with an odd expression in his face, "Simonne was in a great anxiety about you, mademoiselle," said he; "she is not yet come in. Your grandmamma is upstairs as usual. Have you had a pleasant walk?"

Patty made no answer; she ran upstairs quickly. "I must not stay long," she said to herself. "I wonder if Rémy is there." The front door was open, and she went in, and then along the passage, and with a beating heart she stopped and knocked at her grandmother's door. "Come in child," the old lady called out from the inside; and as Patty nervously fumbled at the handle, the voice inside added, "Lift up the latch, and the hasp will fall. Come in," and Patty went in as she was told.

It was getting to be a little dark in-doors by this time, and the room seemed to Patty full of an odd dazzle of light — perhaps because the glass door of the dressing-closet, in which many of Madame Capuchon's stores were kept, was open.

"Come here, child," said her grandmother, hoarsely, "and let me look at you."

"How hoarsely you speak!" said Patty; "I'm afraid your cold is very bad, grandmamma."

The old lady grunted and shook her head. "My health is miserable at all times," she said. "What is that you have got in your basket? butter, is it not, by the smell?"

"What a good nose you have, grandmamma," said Patty, laughing, and opening her basket. "I have brought you a little pat of butter and some honeycomb, with mamma's love," said Patty. "They will supply you from the hotel, if you like, at the same price you pay now."

"Thank you, child," said Madame Capuchon. "Come a little closer and let me look at you. Why, what is the matter? You are all sorts of colors, — blue, green, red. What have you been doing, miss? See if you can find my spectacles on that table."

"What do you want them for, grandmamma?" Patty asked, fumbling about among all the various little odds and ends.

"The better to see you, my dear, and anybody else who may call upon me," said the grandmamma, in her odd broken English. Patty was nervous still and confused, longing to ask whether Rémy had made his appearance, and not daring to speak his name first, and in her confusion she knocked over a little odd-shaped box that was upon the table, and it opened and something fell out.

"Be careful, child! What have you done?" said the old lady, sharply. "Here, give me the things to me."

"It's — it's something made of ivory, grandmamma," said stupid Patty, looking up, bewildered. "What is it for?"

"Take care; take care. Those are my teeth, child. I cannot eat comfortably without them," said the old lady, pettishly. "And now I want to talk seriously. Here, give me your hand, and look me in the face, and tell me honestly what you think of a certain — "

But at that instant a loud ring at the bell was heard, and voices in the passage; the door of the room flew open, and Mrs. Maynard rushed in, burst into a flood of tears, and clasped her daughter to her beating heart.

"I tell you she is here, monsieur," Simonne was saying to Maynard himself, who was following his wife. As soon as he saw her there, with Patty in her arms, "Now, Marthe," he said, "you will at last believe what a goose you are at times;" and he began to laugh in a superior sort of fashion, and then he choked oddly, and sat down with his face hidden in his hands.

"But what is it all about?" asked Madame Capuchon, from her bed.

Poor people! They could hardly own or tell or speak the thought which had been in their minds, so horrible and so absurd as it now seemed. They tried to pass it over; and, indeed, they never owned to one another what that ten minutes' drive had been.

It was all over now, and Patty, in penitent tears, was confessing what had detained her. They could not be angry at such a time, they could only clasp her in their loving arms. All the little miniatures were looking on from their hooks on the wall; the old grandmother was shaking her frills in excitement, and nodding and blinking encouragement from her alcove.

"Look here, Henry," said she to her son-in-law. "I have seen the young man, and I think he is a very fine young fellow. In fact, he is now waiting in the dining-room, for I sent him away when I heard la petite coming. I wanted to talk to her alone. Félicie has written to me on the subject of their union; he wishes it, I wish it, Patty

wishes it. Oh, I can read little girls' faces!
He has been called to the bar. My property
will remain undivided. Why do you oppose
their marriage? I cannot conceive what
objection you can ever have had to it."
"What objection!" said the 'squire, astounded. "Why, you yourself warned me.
Félicie writes as usual with an eye to her
own interest — a grasping, covetous — "
"Hush, hush dear!" interceded Mrs. Maynard, gently pushing her husband towards
the door. The old lady's hands and frills
were trembling more and more by this time;
she was not used to being thwarted; the
'squire also was accustomed to have his own
way.

"My Félicie, my poor child, I cannot suffer her to be spoken of in this way," cried
Madame Capuchon, who at another time
would have been the first to complain.

"Patty is only sixteen," hazarded Mrs.
Maynard.

"I was sixteen when I married," said
Madame Capuchon.

"Patty shall wait till she is sixty-six
before I give her to a penniless adventurer,"
cried the 'squire in great wrath.

"Very well," said the old lady, spitefully.
"Now I will tell you what I have told him.
As I tell you, he came to see me just now,
and is at this moment, I believe, devouring
the remains of the pie Simonne prepared
for your luncheon. I have told him that he
shall be my heir whether you give him Patty
or not. I am not joking, Henry; I mean it.
I like the young man exceedingly. He is an
extremely well-bred young fellow, and will
do us all credit."

Maynard shrugged his shoulders and
looked at his wife.

"But, child, do you really care for him?"
Patty's mother said, reproachfully. "What
can you know of him?" and she took both
the little hands in hers.

Little Patty hung her head for a minute.
"O mamma, he has told me everything;
he told me he did think of the money at
first, but only before he knew me. Dear
papa, if you talked to him you would believe
him, indeed you would, — indeed, indeed you
would." Patty's imploring, wistful glance
touched the 'squire, and as she said, Maynard could not help believing in Rémy when
he came to talk things over quietly with
him, and without losing his temper.

He found him in the dining-room, with a
bottle of wine and the empty pie-dish before him; the young man had finished off
everything but the bones and the cork and
the bottle. "I had no breakfast, sir," said
Rémy, starting up, half laughing, half
ashamed. "My grandmother told me to
look in the cupboard."

"Such a good appetite should imply a
good conscience," Maynard thought; and at
last he relented, and eventually grew to be
very fond of his son-in-law.

Patty and Rémy were married on her sev-
enteenth birthday. I first saw them in the
court-yard of the hotel, but afterwards at
Sunnymede, where they spent last summer.
Madame Capuchon is not yet satisfied
with the butter. It is a very difficult thing
to get anywhere good. Simonne is as devoted as ever, and tries hard to satisfy her
mistress.

THE

SLEEPING BEAUTY IN THE WOOD.

BY

MISS THACKERAY,

AUTHOR OF "BEAUTY AND THE BEAST," "LITTLE RED RIDING HOOD," "JACK THE
GIANT-KILLER," "CINDERELLA," ETC.

LORING, Publisher,
319 WASHINGTON STREET,
BOSTON.
1867.

THE SLEEPING BEAUTY IN THE WOOD.

A KIND enchantress one day put into my hand a mystic volume prettily lettered and bound in green, saying, " I am so fond of this book. It has all the dear old fairy tales in it; one never tires of them. Do take it." I carried the little book away with me, and spent a very pleasant, quiet evening at home by the fire, with H. at the opposite corner, and other old friends, whom I felt I had somewhat neglected of late. Jack and the Beanstalk, Puss in Boots, the gallant and quixotic Giant-killer, and dearest Cinderella, whom we every one of us must have loved, I should think, ever since we first knew her in her little brown pinafore : I wondered, as I shut them all up for the night between their green boards, what it was that made these stories so fresh and so vivid. Why did not they fall to pieces, vanish, explode, disappear, like so many of their contemporaries and descendants ? And yet, far from being forgotten and passing away, it would seem as if each generation in turn, as it came into the world, looks to be delighted still by the brilliant pageant, and never tires or wearies of it. And on their side princes and princesses never seem to grow any older; the castles and the lovely gardens flourish without need of repair or whitewash, or plumbers or glaziers. The princesses' gowns, too, — sun, moon, and star color, — do not wear out or pass out of fashion or require altering. Even the seven-leagued boots do not appear to be the worse for wear. Numbers of realistic stories for children have passed away. Little Henry and his Bearer, Poor Harry and Lucy, have very nearly given up their little artless ghosts and prattle, and ceased making their own beds for the instruction of less excellently brought up little boys and girls ; and, notwithstanding a very interesting article in the *Saturday Review*, it must be owned that Harry Sandford and Tommy Merton are not familiar playfellows in our nurseries and school-rooms, and have passed somewhat out of date. But not so all these centenarians, — Prince Riquet, Carabas, Little Red Riding-hood, Bluebeard, and others. They seem as if they would never grow old. They play with the children, they amuse the elders, there seems no end to their fund of spirits and perennial youth.

H., to whom I made this remark, said, from the opposite chimney-corner, " No wonder; the stories are only histories of real, living persons turned into fairy princes and princesses. Fairy stories are everywhere and every day. We are all princes and princesses in disguise, or ogres or wicked dwarfs. All these histories are the histories of human nature, which does not seem to change very much in a thousand years or so, and we don't get tired of the fairies because they are so true to it."

After this little speech of H.'s, we spent an unprofitable half-hour reviewing our acquaintance, and classing them under their real characters and qualities. We had dined with Lord Carabas only the day before, and met Puss in Boots ; Beauty and the Beast were also there. We uncharitably counted up, I am ashamed to say, no less than six Bluebeards. Jack and the Beanstalk we had met just starting on his climb. A Red Riding-hood ; a girl with toads dropping from her mouth : we knew three or four of each. Cinderellas — alas ! who does not know more than one dear, poor, pretty Cinderella ; and as for sleeping princesses in the woods, how many one can reckon up ! Young, old, ugly, pretty, awakening, sleeping still.

"Do you remember Cecilia Lulworth," said H., " and Dorlicote ? Poor Cecilia ! "

Some lives are *couleur de rose*, people say ; others seem to be, if not *couleur de rose* all through, yet full of bright, beautiful tints, blues, pinks, little bits of harmonious cheerfulness. Other lives, if not so brilliant, and seeming more or less gray at times, are very sweet and gentle in tone, with faint gleams of gold or lilac to brighten them. And then again others, alas ! are black and

8

hopeless from the beginning. Besides these, there are some which have always appeared to me as if they were of a dark, dull hue; a dingy, heavy brown, which no happiness, or interest, or bright color could ever enliven. Blues turn sickly, roses seem faded, and yellow lilacs look red and ugly upon these heavy backgrounds. Poor Cecilia, — as H. called her, — hers had always seemed to me one of these latter existences, unutterably dull, commonplace, respectable, stinted, ugly, and useless.

Lulworth Hall, with the great, dark park bounded by limestone walls, with iron gates here and there, looked like a blot upon the bright and lovely landscape. The place from a distance, compared with the surrounding country, was a blur and a blemish as it were, — sad, silent, solitary.

Travellers passing by sometimes asked if the place was uninhabited, and were told, "No, shure, — fam'ly lives thear all the yeaurr round." Some charitable souls might wonder what life could be like behind those dull gates. One day a young fellow riding by saw rather a sweet woman's face gazing for an instant through the bars, and he went on his way with a momentary thrill of pity. Need I say that it was poor Cecilia who looked out vacantly to see who was passing along the high-road. She was surrounded by hideous moreen, oil-cloth, punctuality, narrow-mindedness, horsehair, and mahogany. Loud bells rang at intervals, regular, monotonous. Surly but devoted attendants waited upon her. She was rarely alone; her mother did not think it right that a girl in Cecilia's position should "race" about the grounds unattended; as for going outside the walls it was not to be thought of. When Cecilia went out with her gloves on, and her goloshes, her mother's companion, Miss Bowley, walked beside her up and down the dark laurel walk at the back of the house, — up and down, down and up, up and down. "I think I am getting tired, Maria," Miss Lulworth would say at last. "If so we had better return to the hall," Maria would reply, "although it is before our time." And then they would walk home in silence, between the iron railings and laurel-bushes.

As Cecilia walked erectly by Miss Bowley's side, the rooks went whirling over their heads, the slugs crept sleepily along the path under the shadow of the grass and the weeds; they heard no sounds except the cawing of the birds, and the distant mo-

notonous, hacking noise of the gardener and his boy digging in the kitchen-garden.

Cecilia, peeping into the long drab drawing-room on her return, might, perhaps, see her mother, erect and dignified, at her open desk, composing, writing, crossing, re-reading, an endless letter to an indifferent cousin in Ireland, with a single candle and a small piece of blotting-paper, and a pen-wiper made of ravellings, all spread out before her.

"You have come home early, Cecil," says the lady, without looking up. "You had better make the most of your time, and practise till the dressing-bell rings. Maria will kindly take up your things."

And then in the chill twilight Cecilia sits down to the jangling instrument, with the worn silk flutings. A faded rack it is upon which her fingers had been distended ever since she can remember. A great many people think there is nothing in the world so good for children as scoldings, whippings, dark cupboards, and dry bread and water, upon which they expect them to grow up into tall, fat, cheerful, amiable men and women; and a great many people think that for grown-up young people the silence, the chillness, the monotony and sadness of their own fading twilight days is all that is required. Mrs. Lulworth and Maria Bowley, her companion, Cecilia's late governess, were quite of this opinion. They themselves, when they were little girls, had been slapped, snubbed, locked up in closets, thrust into bed at all sorts of hours, flattened out on backboards, set on high stools to play the piano for days together, made to hem frills five or six weeks long, and to learn immense pieces of poetry, so that they had to stop at home all the afternoon. And though Mrs. Lulworth had grown up stupid, suspicious, narrow-minded, soured, and overbearing, and had married for an establishment, and Miss Bowley, her governess's daughter, had turned out nervous, undecided, melancholy, and anxious, and had never married at all, yet they determined to bring up Cecilia as they themselves had been brought up, and sincerely thought they could not do better.

When Mrs. Lulworth married, she said to Maria, "You must come and live with me, and help to educate my children some day, Maria. For the present I shall not have a home of my own; we are going to reside with my husband's aunt, Mrs. Dormer. She is a very wealthy person, far advanced in years. She is greatly annoyed with Mr.

and Mrs. John Lulworth's vagaries, and she has asked me and my husband to take their places at Dorlicote Hall." At the end of ten years Mrs. Lulworth wrote again: "We are now permanently established in our aunt's house. I hear you are in want of a situation; pray come and superintend the education of my only child, Cecilia (she is named after her godmother, Mrs. Dormer). She is now nearly three years old, and I feel that she begins to require some discipline."

This letter was written at that same desk twenty-two years before Cecilia began her practising that autumn evening. She was twenty-five years old now, but like a child in inexperience, in ignorance, in placidity; a fortunate stolidity and slowness of temperament had saved her from being crushed and nipped in the bud, as it were. She was not bored because she had never known any other life. It seemed to her only natural that all days should be alike, rung in and out by the jangling breakfast, lunch, dinner, and prayer-bells. Mr. Dormer — a little chip of a man — read prayers suitable for every day in the week; the servants filed in, maids first, then the men. Once Cecilia saw one of the maids blush and look down smiling as she marched out after the others. Miss Dormer wondered a little, and thought she would ask Susan why she looked so strangely; but Susan married the groom soon after, and went away, and Cecilia never had an opportunity of speaking to her.

Night after night Mr. Dormer replaced his spectacles with a click, and pulled up his shirt-collar when the service was ended. Night after night old Mrs. Dormer coughed a little moaning cough. If she spoke, it was generally to make some little, bitter remark. Every night she shook hands with her nephew and niece, kissed Cecilia's blooming cheek, and patted out of the room. She was a little woman with starling eyes. She had never got over her husband's death. She did not always know when she moaned. She dressed in black, and lived alone in her turret, where she had various old-fashioned occupations, — tatting, camphor-boxes to sort, a real old spinning-wheel and distaff among other things, at which Cecilia, when she was a child, had pricked her fingers trying to make it whirr as her aunt did. Spinning-wheels have quite gone out, but I know of one or two old ladies who still use them. Mrs. Dormer would go nowhere, and would see no one.

So at least her niece, the master-spirit, declared, and the old lady got to believe it at last. I don't know how much the fear of the obnoxious John and his wife and children may have had to do with this arrangement.

When her great aunt was gone it was Cecilia's turn to gather her work together at a warning sign from her mother, and walk away through the long, chilly passages to her slumbers in the great green four-post bed. And so time passed. Cecilia grew up. She had neither friends nor lovers. She was not happy nor unhappy. She could read, but she never cared to open a book. She was quite contented; for she thought Lulworth Hall the finest place, and its inmates the most important people in the world. She worked a great deal, embroidering interminable quilts and braided toilet-covers and fish-napkins. She never thought of anything but the utterest commonplaces and platitudes. She considered that being respectable and decorous, and a little pompous and overbearing, was the duty of every well-brought-up lady and gentleman. To-night she banged away very placidly at Rhodes' air, for the twentieth time breaking down in the same passage and making the same mistake, until the dressing-bell rang, and Cecilia, feeling she had done her duty, then extinguished her candle, and went upstairs across the great, chill hall, up the bare oil-cloth gallery, to her room.

Most young women have some pleasure, whatever their troubles may be, in dressing, and pretty trinkets and beads and ribbons and necklaces. An unconscious love of art and intuition leads some of them, even plain ones, to adorn themselves. The colors and ribbon ends brighten bright faces, enliven dull ones, deck what is already lovable, or, at all events, make the most of what materials there are. Even a Maypole, crowned and flowered and tastily ribboned, is a pleasing object. And, indeed, the art of decoration seems to me a charming natural instinct, and one which is not nearly enough encouraged, and a gift which every woman should try to acquire. Some girls, like birds, know how to weave, out of ends of rags, of threads and morsels and straws, a beautiful whole, a work of real genius for their habitation. Frivolities, say some; waste of time, say others, — expense, vanity. The strong-minded dowagers shake their heads at it all, — Mrs. Lulworth among them; only why had Nature painted Cecilia's cheeks of brightest pink, instead of bilious orange, like poor Maria Bowley's? why was her hair all crisp and curly? and were her white, even teeth, and her clear, gray eyes, vanity and frivolity too? Cecilia was rather too stout for her age; she had not much expression in her face. And no wonder. There was not much to be expressive about in her poor little stinted life. She could not go into raptures over the mahogany sideboard, the camphene lamp in the drawing-room, the four-post beds indoors, the laurel-bushes without, the Moorish temple with yellow glass windows, or the wigwam summer-house, which were the alternate boundaries of her daily walks.

Cecilia was not allowed a fire to dress herself by; a grim maid, however, attended, and I suppose she was surrounded, as people say, by every comfort. There was a horsehair sofa, everything was large, solid, brown as I have said, grim, and in its place. The rooms at Lulworth Hall did not take the impress of their inmate; the inmate was moulded by the room. There were in Cecilia's no young lady-like trifles lying here and there; upon the chest of drawers there stood a mahogany workbox, square, with a key, — that was the only attempt at feminine elegance, — a little faded chenille, I believe, was to be seen round the clock on the chimney-piece, and a black and white check dressing-gown and an ugly little pair of slippers were set out before the toilet-table. On the bed, Cecilia's dinner-costume was lying, — a sickly green dress, trimmed with black, — and a white flower for her hair. On the toilet-table an old-fashioned jasper serpent-necklace and a set of amethysts were displayed for her to choose from, also mittens and a couple of hair-bracelets. The girl was quite content, and she would go down gravely to dinner, smoothing out her hideous toggery.

Mrs. Dormer never came down before dinner. All day long she stayed up in her room, dozing and trying remedies, and occasionally looking over old journals and letters until it was time to come downstairs. She liked to see Cecilia's pretty face at one side of the table, while her nephew carved, and Mrs. Lulworth recounted any of the stirring events of the day. She was used to the life, — she was sixty when they came to her, she was long past eighty now, — the last twenty years had been like a long sleep, with the dream of what happened when she was alive and in the world continually passing before her.

When the Lulworths first came to her she had been in a low and nervous state, only stipulated for quiet and peace, and that no one was to come to her house of mourning. The John Lulworths, a cheery couple, broke down at the end of a month or two, and preferred giving up all chance of their aunt's great inheritance to living in such utter silence and seclusion. Upon Charles, the younger brother and his wife, the habit had grown, until now anything else would have been toil and misery to them. Except the old rector from the village, the doctor now and then, no other human creature ever crossed the threshold. For Cecilia's sake Miss Bowley once ventured to hint, —

"Cecilia with her expectations has the whole world before her."

"Maria!" said Mrs. Lulworth, severely; and, indeed, to this foolish woman it seemed as if money would add more to her daughter's happiness than the delights, the wonders, the interests, the glamours of youth. Charles Lulworth, shrivelled, selfish, dull, worn-out, did not trouble his head about Cecilia's happiness, and let his wife do as she liked with the girl.

This especial night when Cecilia came down in her ugly green dress, it seemed to her as if something unusual had been going on. The old lady's eyes looked bright and glittering, her father seemed more animated than usual, her mother looked mysterious and put out. It might have been fancy, but Cecilia thought they all stopped talking as she came into the room; but then dinner was announced, and her father offered Mrs. Dormer his arm immediately, and they went into the dining-room.

It must have been fancy. Everything was as usual. "They have put up a few hurdles in Dalron's field, I see," said Mrs. Lulworth. "Charles, you ought to give orders for repairing the lock of the harness-room."

"Have they seen to the pump-handle?" said Mr. Lulworth.

"I think not." And then there was a dead silence.

"Potatoes," said Cecilia, to the footman. "Mamma, we saw ever so many slugs in the laurel walk, Maria and I, — didn't we, Maria? I think there are a great many slugs in our place."

Old Mrs. Dormer looked up while Cecilia was speaking, and suddenly interrupted her in the middle of her sentence. "How old are you, child?" she said; "are you seventeen or eighteen?"

"Eighteen! Aunt Cecilia. I am five-and-twenty," said Cecilia, staring.

"Good gracious! Is it possible?" said her father, surprised.

"Cecil is a woman now," said her mother. "Five-and-twenty!" said the old lady, quite crossly. "I had no idea time went so fast. She ought to have been married long ago; that is, if she means to marry at all." "Pray, my dear aunt, do not put such ideas—" Mrs. Lulworth began.

"I don't intend to marry," said Cecilia, peeling an orange, and quite unmoved, and she slowly curled the rind of her orange in the air. "I think people are very stupid to marry. Look at poor Jane Simmonds; her husband beats her; Jones saw her."

"So you don't intend to marry?" said the old lady, with an odd inflection in her voice. "Young ladies were not so wisely brought up in my early days," and she gave a great sigh. "I was reading an old letter this morning from your poor father, Charles, —all about happiness, and love in a cot, and two little curly-headed boys,—Jack, you know, and yourself. I should rather like to see John again."

"What, my dear aunt, after his unparalleled audacity? I declare the thought of his impudent letter makes my blood boil," exclaimed Mrs. Lulworth.

"Does it?" said the old lady. "Cecilia, my dear, you must know that your uncle has discovered that the entail was not cut off from a certain property which my father left me, and which I brought to my husband. He has therefore written me a very business-like letter, in which he says he wishes for no alteration at present, but begs that, in the event of my making my will, I should remember this, and not complicate matters by leaving it to yourself, as had been my intention. I see nothing to offend in the request. Your mother thinks differently."

Cecilia was so amazed at being told anything that she only stared again, and, opening a wide mouth, popped into it such a great piece of orange that she could not speak for some minutes.

"Cecilia has certainly attained years of discretion," said her great-aunt; "she does not compromise herself by giving any opinion on matters she does not understand."

Notwithstanding her outward imperturbability, Cecilia was a little stirred and interested by this history, and by the little conversation which had preceded it. Her mother was sitting upright in her chair as usual, netting with vigorous action; her large foot outstretched, her stiff, bony hands

working and jerking monotonously. Her father was dozing in his arm-chair. Old Mrs. Dormer, too, was nodding in her corner. The monotonous Maria was stitching in the lamplight. Gray and black shadows loomed all round her. The far end of the room was quite dark; the great curtains swept from their ancient cornices. Cecilia, for the first time in all her life, wondered whether she should ever live all her life in this spot, —ever go away? It seemed impossible, unnatural, that she should ever do so. Silent, dull as it was, she was used to it, and did not know what was amiss. . . .

Young Frank Lulworth, the lawyer of the family—John Lulworth's eldest son—it was who had found it all out. His father wrote that with Mrs. Dormer's permission he proposed coming down in a day or two to show her the papers, and to explain to her personally how the matter stood. "My son and I," said John Lulworth, "both feel that this would be far more agreeable to our feelings, and perhaps to yours, than having recourse to the usual professional intervention; for we have no desire to press our claims for the present; and we only wish that in the ultimate disposal of your property you should be aware how the matter really stands. We have always been led to suppose that the estate actually in question has been long destined by you for your grand-niece, Cecilia Lulworth. I hear from our old friend, Dr. Hicks, that she is remarkably pretty and very amiable. Perhaps such vague possibilities are best unmentioned; but it has occurred to me that in the event of a mutual understanding springing up between the young folks, — my son and your grand-niece, — the connection might be agreeable to us all, and lead to a renewal of that family intercourse which has been, to my great regret, suspended for some time past."

Old Mrs. Dormer, in her shaky Italian handwriting, answered her nephew's letter by return of post: —

"My dear Nephew, —I must acknowledge the receipt of your epistle of the 13th instant. By all means invite your son to pay us his proposed visit. We can then talk over business matters at our leisure, and young Francis can be introduced to his relatives. Although a long time has elapsed since we last met, believe me, my dear nephew, not unmindful of by-gone associations, and yours, very truly, always,

"C. Dormer."

The letter was in the postman's bag when old Mrs. Dormer informed Mrs. Charles of what she had done.

Frank Lulworth thought that in all his life he had never seen anything so dismal, so silent, so neglected, as Dorlicote Park, when he drove up, a few days after, through the iron gates and along the black laurel wilderness which led to the house. The laurel branches, all unpruned, untrained, were twisting savagely in and out, wreathing and interlacing one another, clutching tender shootings, wrestling with the young oak-trees and the limes. He passed by black and sombre avenues leading to mouldy temples, to crumbling summer-houses; he saw what had once been a flower-garden, now all run to seed, — wild, straggling, forlorn; a broken-down bench, a heap of hurdles lying on the ground, a field-mouse darting across the road, a desolate autumn sun shining upon all this mouldering ornament and confusion. It seemed more forlorn and melancholy by contrast, somehow, coming as he did out of the loveliest country and natural sweetness into the dark and tangled wilderness within these limestone walls of Dorlicote.

The parish of Dorlicote-cum-Rockington looks prettier in the autumn than at any other time. A hundred crisp tints, jewelled rays, — grays, browns, purples, glinting golds, and silvers, — rustle and sparkle upon the branches of the nut-trees, of the bushes and thickets. Soft blue mists and purple tints rest upon the distant hills; scarlet berries glow among the brown leaves of the hedges; lovely mists fall and vanish suddenly, revealing bright and sweet autumnal sights; blackberries, stacks of corn, brown leaves crisping upon the turf, great pears hanging sweetening in the sun over the cottage lintels, cows grazing and whisking their tails, blue smoke curling from the tall farm chimneys; all is peaceful, prosperous, golden. You can see the sea on clear days from certain knolls and hillocks. . . . .

Out of all these pleasant sights young Lulworth came into this dreary splendor. He heard no sounds of life, — he saw no one. His coachman had opened the iron gate. "They doan't keep no one to moind the gate," said the driver; "only tradesmen cooms to th'ouse." Even the gardener and his boy were out of the way; and when they got sight of the house at last, many of the blinds were down and shutters shut, and only two chimneys were smoking. There was some one living in the place, however, for a watch-dog who was lying asleep in his kennel woke up and gave a heart-rending howl when Frank got out and rang at the bell.

He had to wait an immense time before anybody answered, although a little page in buttons came and stared at him in blank amazement from one of the basement windows, and never moved. Through the same window Frank could see into the kitchen, and he was amused when a little cook came up behind the little page and languidly boxed his ears, and seemed to order him off the premises.

The butler, who at last answered the door, seemed utterly taken aback, — nobody had called for months past, and here was a perfect stranger taking out his card, and asking for Mrs. Dormer, as if it was the most natural thing in the world. The under-butler was half-asleep in his pantry, and had not heard the door-bell. The page — the very same whose ears had been boxed — came wondering to the door, and went to ascertain whether Mrs. Dormer would see the gentleman or not.

"What a vault, what a catacomb, what an ugly old place!" thought Frank, as he waited. He heard steps far, far away; then came a long silence, and then a heavy tread slowly approaching, and the old butler beckoned to him to follow, — through a cobweb-color room, through a brown room, through a gray room, into a great, dim, drab drawing-room, where the old lady was sitting alone. She had come down her back stairs to receive him; it was years since she had left her room before dinner.

Even old ladies look kindly upon a tall, well-built, good-looking, good-humored young man. Frank's nose was a little too long, his mouth a little too straight; but he was a handsome young fellow, with a charming manner. Only, as he came up, he was somewhat shy and undecided, — he did not know exactly how to address the old lady. This was his great-aunt. He knew nothing whatever about her, but she was very rich; she had invited him to come, and she had a kind face, he thought; should he, — ought he to embrace her? Perhaps he ought, and he made the slightest possible movement in this direction. Mrs. Dormer, divining his object, pushed him weakly away. "How do you do? No embraces, thank you. I don't care for kissing at my age. Sit down, — there, in that chair opposite, — and now tell me about your father, and all the family, and about this ridiculous discovery of yours. I don't believe a word of it."

The interview between them was long and satisfactory on the whole. The unconscious Cecilia and Miss Bowley returned that afternoon from their usual airing, and, as it happened, Cecilia said, "O Maria! I left my mittens in the drawing-room last night. I will go and fetch them." And, little thinking of what was awaiting her, she flung open the door and marched in through the ante-room, — mushroom hat and brown veil, goloshes and dowdy gown, as usual. "What is this?" thought young Lulworth; "why, who would have supposed it was such a pretty girl?" for suddenly the figure stopped short, and a lovely, fresh face looked up in utter amazement out of the hideous disguise.

"There, don't stare, child," said the old lady. "This is Francis Lulworth, a very intelligent young man, who has got hold of your fortune and ruined all your chances, my dear. He wanted to embrace me just now. Francis, you may as well salute your cousin instead: she is much more of an age for such compliments," said Mrs. Dormer, waving her hand.

The impassive Cecilia, perfectly bewildered, and not in the least understanding, only turned her great, sleepy, astonished eyes upon her cousin, and stood perfectly still as if she was one of those beautiful wax-dolls one sees stuck up to be stared at. If she had been surprised before, utter consternation can scarcely convey her state of mind when young Lulworth stepped up and obeyed her aunt's behest. And, indeed, a stronger-minded person than Cecilia might have been taken aback, who had come into the drawing-room to fetch her mittens, and was met in such an astounding fashion. Frank, half laughing, half kindly, seeing that Cecilia stood quite still and stared at him, supposed it was expected, and did as he was told.

The poor girl gave one gasp of horror, and blushed for the first time, I believe, in the course of her whole existence. Bowley, fixed and open-mouthed from the inner room, suddenly fled with a scream, which recalled Cecilia to a sense of outraged propriety; for, blushing and blinking more deeply, she at last gave three little sobs, and then, O horror! burst into tears!

"Highty-tighty! what a much ado about nothing!" said the old lady, losing her temper and feeling not a little guilty, and much alarmed as to what her niece Mrs. Lul-

worth might say were she to come on the scene.

"I beg your pardon. I am so very, very sorry," said the young man, quite confused and puzzled. "I ought to have known better. I frightened you. I am your cousin, you know, and really,—pray, pray excuse my stupidity," he said, looking anxiously into the fair, placid face along which the tears were coursing in two streams, like a child's.

"Such a thing never happened in all my life before," said Cecilia. "I know it is wrong to cry, but really — really—"

"Leave off crying directly, miss," said her aunt, testily, "and let us have no more of this nonsense." The old lady dreaded the mother's arrival every instant. Frank, half laughing, but quite unhappy at the poor girl's distress, had taken up his hat to go that minute, not knowing what else to do.

"Ah! you're going," says old Mrs. Dormer; "no wonder. Cecilia, you have driven your cousin away by your rudeness."

"I'm not rude," sobbed Cecilia. "I can't help crying."

"The girl is a greater idiot than I took her for," cried the old lady. "She has been kept here locked up until she has not a single idea left in her silly noddle. No man of sense could endure her for five minutes. You wish to leave the place, I see, and no wonder!"

"I really think," said Frank, "that under the circumstances it is the best thing I can do. Miss Lulworth, I am sure, would wish me to go."

"Certainly," said Cecilia. "Go away, pray go away. Oh, how silly I am!"

Here was a catastrophe!

The poor old fairy was all puzzled and bewildered: her arts were powerless in this emergency. The princess had awakened, but in tears. The prince still stood by, distressed and concerned, feeling horribly guilty, and yet scarcely able to help laughing. Poor Cecilia! her aunt's reproaches had only bewildered her more and more; and for the first time in her life she was bewildered, discomposed, forgetful of hours. It was the hour of calisthenics; but Miss Lulworth forgot everything that might have been expected from a young lady of her admirable bringing-up.

Fairy tales are never very long, and this one ought to come to an end. The princess was awake now; her simplicity and beauty

2

touched the young prince, who did not, I think, really intend to go, though he took up his hat.

Certainly the story would not be worth the telling if they had not been married soon after, and lived happily all the rest of their lives.

It is not in fairy tales only that things fall out as one could wish, and, indeed, H. and T. agreed the other night that fairies, although invisible, had not entirely vanished out of the land.

It is certainly like a fairy transformation to see Cecilia nowadays in her own home with her children and husband about her. Bright, merry, full of sympathy and interest, she seems to grow prettier every minute.

When Frank fell in love with her and proposed, old Mrs. Dormer insisted upon instantly giving up the Dorlicote Farm for the young people to live in. Mr. and Mrs. Frank Lulworth are obliged to live in London, but they go there every summer with their children; and for some years after her marriage, Cecilia's godmother, who took the opportunity of the wedding to break through many of her recluse habits, used to come and see her every day in a magnificent yellow chariot.

Some day I may perhaps tell you more about the fairies and enchanting princesses of my acquaintance.